A Crime Well Versed

Marlene Chase

AnniesFiction.com

Books in the Secrets of the Castleton Manor Library series

A Crime Well Versed
Copyright © 2017, 2021 Annie's.

Library of Congress-in-Publication Data
A Crime Well Versed/ by Marlene Chase
p. cm.
I. Title
                    2017954734

AnniesFiction.com
(800) 282-6643
Secrets of the Castleton Manor Library™
Series Creator: Shari Lohner
Series Editor: Lorie Jones
Cover Illustrator: Jesse Reisch

10 11 12 13 14 | Printed in China | 9 8 7 6 5 4 3

"It's probably best if you wait in the car, Watson," Faith Newberry said as she parked in front of Happy Tails Gourmet Bakery.

The black-and-white cat leaped expectantly toward the door, whiskers twitching.

"Don't worry. You'll get your tunaroons." The tuna-flavored macaroons were a specialty of the bakery and Watson's favorite.

She petted the handsome tuxedo cat, who had been her companion since she'd rescued him from behind a snow-covered Dumpster in Boston. He'd made the move to Lighthouse Bay on Cape Cod with ease when she accepted the position of librarian at Castleton Manor, an exclusive mansion retreat for booklovers.

A gust of April wind whipped her chestnut hair as she emerged onto Main Street. Faith stopped to gaze at the lighthouse overlooking the ocean. She never tired of the magnificent view—the bobbing boats in the harbor and the great swell of water with its astonishing palette of color. Today, more gray than blue, the ocean reflected a slate sky through which a pale sun penetrated.

The bell jingled when Faith entered the bakery.

"Top of the morning to ya," exulted Midge Foster, green eyes dancing. The owner of Happy Tails flashed a brilliant fuchsia smile. "Don't tell me Watson's already eaten all those tunaroons you bought last week."

Faith laughed. "Yes, I'm afraid he's all out."

"Well, we can fix that problem. Like my daddy always said, 'Ain't nothin' easy, but hard is what we do best,'" Midge drawled. She was originally from Frog Eye, Alabama, and sometimes she still slipped into her distinctive Southern accent.

Faith counted the concierge veterinarian and entrepreneur among her closest friends. Like Faith, Midge was a member of the Candle House Book Club, overseen by Eileen Piper, Faith's aunt and head librarian of Lighthouse Bay's privately funded library. Pets were welcome at club meetings, as they were at Castleton Manor. Watson frequently accompanied Faith to meetings, and Midge brought Atticus. Midge lavished all her maternal affection on her Chihuahua because her two children were away at college, leaving her nest empty except for Atticus and her husband, Peter.

Faith felt the glow of warm well-being. Her job at Castleton Manor had given her the opportunity not only to bond with her favorite aunt but also to enjoy a very special circle of friends.

"Actually, I was hoping to catch a ride to Castleton." Midge brushed a wispy blonde hair off her forehead with pink-tipped fingers. "I got a request to see about a dog being boarded there, but my car's in the shop."

Many guests of the upscale literary retreat brought their pets with them on vacation. The manor pandered to its four-footed guests, offering certain luxuries and on-site services such as pet acupressure and massage. All the staff members knew Midge and called on her when a guest's pet was in need of her services.

"Of course," Faith said readily. "I've finished my errands, and this was my last stop. I'll be happy to drive you out and bring you back."

Midge gave last-minute instructions to Sarah Goodwin, the manager of the bakery and her most trusted employee. She lifted her coat from behind the counter along with a black medical bag imprinted with her initials in bright purple letters.

The focus of the manor's upcoming retreat was poetry, and a formidable collection of verse aficionados, students, and experts had been gathering. "I haven't met many of the guests or their pets yet," Faith admitted. "It must be something serious to call you out so soon."

"A lethargic Newfoundland that appears to be undernourished and may have symptoms of mange."

"A Newfoundland!" Faith stared at Midge. "But that breed is as big as a pony. I thought Castleton had a rule about the size of pets that are allowed."

"I know. Apparently, some special dispensation has been given. But the staff has isolated him until he's checked out to be sure he doesn't have anything contagious." Midge raised a well-shaped eyebrow. "According to Marlene, it's imperative that I come immediately, and you know how she can be."

"Ah," Faith responded knowingly. Marlene Russell, the manor's assistant manager and Faith's boss, was a stickler for the rules. *Well, usually,* Faith thought. Woe betide anyone who didn't see things her way. Faith and Marlene had had their confrontations, and in the beginning Faith had despaired of ever getting along with her. But she had figured out how to work with her, and she respected the iron lady's organizational abilities and precision.

"What's the big boss been up to these days?" Midge asked as they wended their way toward the manor.

Midge was referring to Wolfe Jaxon, the owner of Castleton Manor and perhaps the most sought-after bachelor in Lighthouse Bay. A direct descendant of the wealthy nineteenth-century whaling captain Angus Jaxon, Wolfe looked after the family's considerable enterprises, which included the retreats for booklovers held in the luxurious mansion.

Faith detected the teasing note in her friend's voice and shrugged. "I believe he's away on business."

Wolfe frequently traveled abroad, but she'd heard rumors that he was expected back in Massachusetts soon. It surprised her how much she hoped the rumors were true, as a vision of the strikingly handsome entrepreneur appeared in her mind—dark hair peppered with gray, eyes as blue and changeful as the ocean. That he seemed to go out of his way to involve himself in matters that concerned her had made her wary at first, but they had become friends.

"He seems to be spending more time at the manor now." Midge glanced at her and smiled meaningfully.

"No he doesn't," Faith countered, feeling heat rise to her face. "And even if he does, it has nothing to do with me." She turned more sharply than necessary onto the private road leading to Castleton Manor. "Is there another sight as magnificent as this?"

While she was anxious to derail conversation from Wolfe, she was quite literally rendered breathless every time she saw the elegant château-style mansion. Perfectly shaped yew hedges and topiaries flanked the edifice, and the Victorian garden beyond stretched luxuriously. Even in winter the garden wore its best vestments, snow lending fairy-tale enchantment to every tree and bush.

Faith tore her gaze away from the stately mansion and veered onto the road leading to the stables and kennels. A fleet of fine horses for guests to ride on the wooded trails grazed in the verdant grass. Beyond were the spotlessly clean kennels providing every comfort for the pampered pet, though most guests preferred to keep their furry friends with them.

Watson was obviously eager to get out of the vehicle. Ears standing up and paws perched on the window ledge, he peered through the glass. A visit to the kennels—to others of his kind—had to be among Watson's favorite outings.

"The isolation kennel is at the south end," Midge said. "If we find mange, I sure hope it's not the contagious type."

"There's more than one kind of mange?" Faith asked.

"Yup. Mange is caused by mites. The most common types are demodectic and sarcoptic. All dogs are susceptible, but when mites begin to overpopulate they can cause skin issues. We can treat the demodectic kind topically, and it clears up fairly quickly. The sarcoptic variety, however, is caused by burrowing mites known as scabies. This is the contagious kind. It can wreak havoc in a canine community."

Faith cringed. "I had no idea."

They got out of the SUV and heard the barking of a few dogs and the distant nickering of the horses in the stables.

Watson shot out as soon as Faith cracked the door and had already disappeared to begin his own adventure that would involve considerable sniffing and rubbing of noses. He was friendly and usually got along well with other pets, but he could also act aloof.

Annie Jennings, one of the young attendants who cared for Castleton's animal population, greeted them. Annie had been raised in upstate New York, but she was partial to cowboy boots and spurs. She was married to a German rancher fifteen years her senior and seemed very happy with her life. "Your patient's that black Newfie with his head on his paws," she told Midge. "His name's Carlo."

Faith knew the breed, but Carlo was the biggest dog she had ever seen. The Newfoundland was a working dog most at home on a farm or on the ice-driven slopes of the country of its origin. Known for its mild manner and gentle temperament, the breed made an excellent pet for someone with the strength to handle it and the space to house it.

She followed Midge and Annie to the far end of the row where the dog lay, his thick body pressed up close to the inner cage. He panted in the morning sunshine and gazed at them through listless brown eyes until Watson wove back and forth in front of the bars. Then the dog raised his mammoth head and watched the cat's coquettish dance.

Faith scooped up Watson in her arms. "I know you want to check him out, but give Midge a chance to get inside. Then I'll put you down. You and I can watch from here, you little tease."

Carlo got up when Midge approached.

"I can't get over how big he is," Faith commented to no one in particular as Watson wriggled free and took a spot inches from the kennel.

The dog had to weigh more than a hundred pounds, and if he stood up on his hind legs, he could easily knock down Midge. For his part, Watson seemed completely unafraid, though perhaps that was because of the bars between them.

"Big and handsome, aren't you?" Midge said, patting the thick, dull fur around the dog's ears. He was completely black, though a few copper hairs mingled in the tangled expanse. The animal stood docile and still, his tail wagging slowly. Midge inspected him carefully, talking softly all the while.

Watson resumed his bold demonstration, prancing back and forth in front of the cage, clearly intrigued by the dog. Faith thought she even detected a low purring sound—as though perhaps the two were communicating. She stepped closer to hear what was going on.

Standing next to Midge, Annie screwed her face into a frown, as if she smelled something unpleasant. "The owner brought Carlo in this morning. Said she'd be back to check on him and that we'd better see he got the best of everything. She promised to return the medical form every guest with an animal is asked to supply 'in due course.' Then she stormed off."

Carlo's owner is a woman? Faith had imagined some big hunter type would own such a dog.

Midge continued her probing and inspecting, then stood and closed her medical bag. "I don't think there's anything to be terribly concerned about. He has the beginnings of demodectic mange—not the bad kind. This animal needs salve, a good brushing, and supplements to perk him up, and he'll be fine." She knelt and ruffled the dog's ears. "Poor fella just needs some TLC."

"You there, what are you doing to Carlo?"

Faith turned around to see who belonged to the shrill voice piercing the air.

A thin, reedy woman trekked down the slope toward the kennels in knee-high boots with delicate heels. She clutched a black cape over her filmy white calf-length dress, which was clearly inadequate for a chilly April day. A heavily beaded bag hung crosswise over her chest. The woman almost looked like a transplant from the Victorian era. She wore white gloves, and her black hair was parted severely in the middle and pulled into a bun at the nape of her neck.

"Uh-oh, that's the owner," Annie muttered under her breath, then stepped away from the enclosure to attend to other duties.

The woman in white, who was probably somewhere in her forties, came to a halt in front of them and glared at Midge through eyes dark as obsidian beneath low-arced brows. She wasn't beautiful, but something in her regal carriage captivated one's attention.

Midge rose to greet her unusual visitor. "I'm Midge Foster, the veterinarian contracted to examine pets brought to Castleton Manor." She held out a slender hand, exhibiting her best Southern belle persona. "I am honored to meet the owner of this sweet animal." She sounded for all the world like Scarlett O'Hara.

The woman ignored Midge's outstretched hand and lifted a pointy chin. "Indeed, Carlo belongs to me. I'm *Miss* Emilie Smythe." She looked down at the dog, who had lifted himself to a sitting position, as though prepared to do her bidding. He watched his mistress, panting tiredly. Miss Smythe frowned, lending a vulnerable quality to her demeanor. "But there's nothing wrong with my Carlo. What have you given him?"

"I haven't given him anything," Midge responded levelly. "But I've recommended some salve to treat his mange. Also, I believe your dog is undernourished, and as for his coat, well . . ." She raised her chin to the level of Miss Smythe's. "Dogs like Carlo need regular brushing. Something I don't think he's been treated to in a while."

Watson took that moment to prance toward the dog, his stub of a tail wiggling. He made a small pirouette and sat down next to one of Carlo's huge forepaws.

"What's that sneaky old cat doing here?" Emilie demanded.

Faith bit back a retort. *Old? Watson has at least eight of his nine lives left. Sneaky? Well, sometimes.* She stepped forward. "Watson is with me. I'm Faith Newberry, the librarian at Castleton Manor. I live on the premises, and I believe Watson is just introducing himself to a new friend."

The woman grimaced, but Faith thought she spotted a hint of curiosity as well—and perhaps a modicum of respect.

Faith had met many unusual people since coming to work at the manor, and this one certainly fit that description. She tried to temper her quick dislike. When people behaved badly, there was usually a reason.

Midge sprang to her defense, still pouring on the Southern charm. "Miss Newberry is known for her literary prowess. She's a highly educated former librarian and archivist from the prestigious Hawarden University. I declare, Castleton Manor is most fortunate to have gained her services."

Emilie pulled a neon blue leash from the antique beaded bag, losing eye contact with Faith only long enough to hook it to the collar of the dog standing obediently at her side. His large head reached her diminutive waist. "We're taking a walk, Carlo and I," she snapped, giving Midge a withering look, "and when we return I expect my dog to get your complete attention and that brushing you say he needs."

She spun on her heel but stopped abruptly and pivoted around. "Librarian, you say?" she asked Faith, who had picked Watson up to prevent him from going after Carlo.

Faith nodded, too stunned by the actions of the strange woman to speak. Watson emitted a low guttural sound quite unlike anything Faith had heard before and squirmed in her arms. She tightened her hold on him, looking for a way to diffuse the tension. "That's a beautiful bag you have. The beadwork is splendid."

Emilie raised an eyebrow, silenced for a few seconds. Then she said, "If you're any kind of librarian, you must be familiar with the works of the illustrious Emily Dickinson." Her body suddenly stilled, and her eyes turned vacant and unfocused as she stood holding the leash. Her shrill voice softened as she recited:

'Why do I love' You, Sir?
Because—
The Wind does not require the Grass
To answer—Wherefore when He pass
She cannot keep Her place.

Recognizing the lines, Faith stared at Emilie. *She actually looks like the famous poet. Dressed in white, black hair drawn severely back, calls her dog Carlo.* It was the name Dickinson had given to the Newfoundland that companioned her for more than fifteen years.

"And if you are acquainted with the famous poet of Amherst, perhaps you know that for many years she was mentored by a prominent literary critic, one Edward Tarkington Smythe, to whom she wrote many letters in the early 1860s, the most prolific period of her career. The only one she trusted more with her poetry was her sister-in-law, Susan."

Anyone who studied American literature and specifically Dickinson's poetry knew this. Faith nodded.

Emilie's pale face suddenly brightened, all trancelike dreaminess gone. "I am Emilie Faye Smythe, great-great-granddaughter of Edward Smythe."

With that, she whirled around and marched toward the rocky bay in the distance, with Carlo trotting behind her.

2

Faith settled into a booth at Snickerdoodles Bakery & Tea Shop to wait for Aunt Eileen. She had left Watson in her cottage and delivered Midge back to her shop after their visit to the kennels. It had been a highly interesting Monday morning—interesting and a little disconcerting—but at least Carlo would be better off now with Midge's attention. Whether Miss Emilie Smythe's demeanor would improve in the coming days was another matter.

"Ah, there you are!" Eileen Piper rushed toward her in fashionable low-heeled shoes with a jacket open over her blue blouse and gray dress pants. At sixty-two, she had a remarkably wrinkle-free complexion and wore her shoulder-length brown hair in an attractive style. Serenity and intelligence bloomed in her features, but it was her blue eyes, sparkling with clarity and wit, that always amazed Faith.

Faith stood to greet her, feeling thankful once again to live in the town where her lively widowed aunt also resided. They had always shared a love of books, especially mysteries, but the bond between them had grown stronger since Faith had moved from Boston to Lighthouse Bay.

"I'm so glad we could meet for lunch," Faith said, giving her aunt a hug. The bakery was next door to the Candle House Library, where Eileen was the head librarian.

"I wouldn't miss the chance to have lunch with my favorite niece." She smiled as she took her seat. "What brings you to town today?"

"Limousine service for Midge." Faith sat down across from her. "Well, actually, I was running some errands that took me to Happy Tails. For Watson's treats, of course. He's such a spoiled cat. Midge needed a ride to Castleton Manor and her SUV was in the shop, so I offered to take her there and bring her back to town."

"I see," Eileen said, perusing the menu. She looked up at Faith. "One of the animals at the manor off his feed?"

"Not exactly. Midge was called out to check on a lethargic dog belonging to one of the retreat guests. She examined the Newfoundland for mange and made sure he wasn't contagious to the other pets."

"I'm surprised the management allowed a guest to bring an animal that size."

"I was too, but for some reason the manor made an exception. The poor dog seemed listless and depressed—if dogs can be depressed. He perked up a little with Watson who showed off in front of his kennel. Watson teased him but in quite a friendly way." Faith shrugged, recalling the camaraderie she had noted between the two animals. "Who says dogs and cats have to be natural enemies?"

"Have you tried that new crab-cake burger with mushrooms?" Eileen pointed to an entry on the left-hand column of her menu.

Faith cringed slightly at the sight of Eileen's knobby index finger. Her aunt's rheumatoid arthritis had to be painful, but she never complained, and she could do amazing things with a skein of yarn. "I've never had crab with mushrooms," Faith answered. "It seems like an odd combination."

Eileen laughed. "Oh, come on. Where's your sense of adventure?"

"I've heard of tofu buffalo wings, but I haven't tried *them* yet either," Faith said with a grin.

"Chicken," Eileen teased.

"I don't feel like chicken today," she said, pretending to misunderstand.

They were still laughing when the waitress arrived with coffee and to take their order.

"Tell me about the sick Newfie," Eileen said after they had ordered BLTs and settled back with their coffee.

"Fortunately, he wasn't contagious, but Midge prescribed some salve to treat his demodectic mange."

"Demo what?"

Faith chuckled. "Midge said it's a common mange that all dogs are susceptible to. It clears up fairly quickly when treated, but the other variety—are you ready for this? Sarcoptic mange. It's caused by burrowing mites, and it's devastating in a canine community."

"Well, you learn something new every day, and I have my niece to thank for today's supplement to my education." Eileen pursed her lips. "But who would bring a dog of that size—and condition—to a poetry retreat?"

Who indeed? "A woman who calls herself Miss Emilie Faye Smythe." The image of the diminutive, white-clad woman imprinted in Faith's mind brought a curiosity along with an odd sense of impending doom. "She claims to be the great-great-granddaughter of Edward Smythe who mentored Emily Dickinson during the most productive writing period of her life."

"Is that so?"

Faith drew a deep breath and let it out slowly. "Funny thing, though. She was wearing a thin white cotton dress—in April! She had this old-fashioned beaded bag across her chest, and her black hair was parted in the middle and pulled into a bun, just like Dickinson's."

Eileen set her coffee cup down with a decisive clack. "Edward Smythe. A minister and a champion of civil rights in the nineteenth century."

"But he's most remembered for his mentorship of Emily Dickinson." These were facts most librarians knew, especially in New England, the poet's home.

"I believe I met this Emilie Smythe several years ago," Eileen said thoughtfully. "Yes, she was living in Providence and approached us about giving a lecture at Candle House. She has a degree from Wellesley, but she has a reputation for being a bit eccentric, maybe even swimming off the deep end."

"Crazy?" Faith queried with surprise.

"It's all that talk about her great-great-grandfather and how she might actually be Dickinson's great-great-granddaughter."

"But there's no evidence for such a claim," Faith protested. "He was Dickinson's mentor. Their relationship wasn't a romantic one, though in earlier studies, some speculated that it was."

Their sandwiches arrived, and Eileen waited until the waitress had walked away before she leaned forward and continued. "Emilie claims she has unpublished letters that prove they were lovers. As far as I know, no one believes they're authentic. Still, she manages to get involved in literary events, conferences, and such. With her money, she can get in most doors. She likes to dress in white and lecture on the famous poet. Her parents were quite wealthy. They were both killed in an avalanche in Switzerland, but they left her an estate on Martha's Vineyard that would knock your socks off."

Eileen had lived in the area all her life and seemed to know the latest scoop. Odd that the sharp-eyed Marlene, who vetted her sources so carefully, would engage Emilie Smythe for the retreat. And did Wolfe know about the peculiar woman's outrageous claims?

"Actually, it was Mr. Smythe's wife who had the money." Eileen's voice turned nostalgic. "Lillian was his second wife, and she changed his fortune with a quick tying of the nuptial knot. She liked to flaunt her wealth and had her husband bowing to her every whim. They had two children, Emilie and a brother just a year or so older. Believe me, Lillian saw that they had the best of everything, and in the end they were left a fortune."

Eileen shook her head, a look of distaste on her expressive face. "Mr. Smythe had a daughter by his first wife who seems to have been left out of the equation. The black sheep, the forgotten stepchild, nothing like Miss Emilie. She owns a bait and tackle shop on the outskirts of town and has a chip on her shoulder the size of Manhattan."

Both women fell silent, eating their lunch. Faith pondered family dynamics that could be so devastating. She felt sorry for Emilie and her half sister. Money too often destroyed relationships.

"So, Emilie's a guest at Castleton Manor," Eileen said. "And the dog?"

"Carlo," Faith supplied quietly. "Like Emily Dickinson's faithful companion for many years."

"I never saw Emilie with a dog." Eileen folded her arms in front of her. "Actually, I haven't heard or seen anything of her in some time. She travels often, sometimes alone and sometimes with that wealthy brother of hers. Getting a Newfie and calling him Carlo would give her one more connection to the famous poet."

"I don't think she treats him much like a beloved companion," Faith said, recalling the dog's dull coat and listless eyes. "Midge told her that dogs like Carlo need regular brushing and that he obviously hadn't been getting it. She was quite severe in her reprimand. You know how Midge feels about animals."

"How did that go over?"

"Not very well. Emilie looked angry, and I expected a small explosion. But she was distracted by Watson who plopped down next to one of the dog's huge paws. Emilie wanted to know what that 'sneaky old cat' was doing there."

"Must have been quite a scene."

"It was. Then I told Emilie that Watson belonged to me and that I was the librarian at Castleton, and she seemed to change focus. That's when she started talking about the poet of Amherst and spouting lines from one of her poems. And then she said she was the great-great-granddaughter of Edward Tarkington Smythe. She could have knocked me over with a feather."

The waitress refilled their cups and cleared their luncheon plates.

"Want any dessert?" Eileen asked.

"Yes, but I better not," Faith said decisively. "Brooke will be cooking up plenty of tempting concoctions for the guests who have been 'eating poetry,' as Mark Strand's line goes." She leaned back against the soft leather booth. "Brooke's been the sous-chef at Castleton for five years, and the reigning consensus is that she's the best one they've ever had. I have to agree."

"And you're the best librarian they've ever had," Eileen said, reaching out to pat Faith's hand. "Have you brushed up on your Dickinson and other major poets?"

"Yes. Marlene gave me a heads-up weeks in advance." Faith grinned sardonically. "The intimation was that my head would roll if I wasn't well prepared."

"She can be grim," Eileen said. "What have you got planned?"

"Tonight I'm giving a lecture on National Poetry Month."

"That'll be a timely introduction to the event happening this month," Eileen remarked. "It's amazing how the celebration has taken off over the years."

Faith nodded. "I'm excited about it. I just hope Emilie Smythe's antics—whatever they might be—won't dampen the enthusiasm."

Eileen suddenly straightened, eyebrows rising. "Well, that's a sight I didn't expect to see. Especially today." She focused on something behind Faith.

Faith followed her aunt's gaze to the front of the bakery. The door opened, ushering in a draft of cold April wind and a woman dressed in yellow fisherman's overalls and a many-pocketed vest from which fishing lures hung willy-nilly. A shabby hat that looked like it might have belonged to Captain Ahab covered frizzy reddish-brown hair streaked with gray. She was probably in her early fifties, with a thick frame, a round tanned face, and stormy eyes. Her lips were thin and sullen, her gait solid and measured.

Faith tried not to stare as the woman barked out an order for coffee. "Someone you know?" she asked, intrigued by her aunt's consternation.

Eileen picked up her coffee cup with both hands. "I know who she is," she said in hushed tones, "but I've never seen her in the bakery before."

"Who is she?" Faith asked, her impatience mounting.

"I don't see her in town very often at all, and she never darkens the door of the library." Eileen took a long sip of her coffee. A wry smile touched her lips. "Fancy seeing her here today just as we were discussing—"

"Aunt Eileen," Faith interrupted, "who is she?"

"That, my dear, is the aforementioned black sheep of the Smythe dynasty—Maggie Haggedorn, Miss Emilie's half sister."

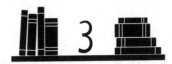

3

The cat leaped onto the back of the couch at the sound of his human approaching the cottage. He'd been cooped up for hours, and despite having a comfortable spot in a sunny window, he was miffed. He wanted to go see the big sad dog again. Normally, he treated canines with the disdain they deserved. The slobbering creatures, always turning cartwheels for their humans and chasing after a ridiculous stick no matter how many times it was thrown. Had they no dignity? But there was something about the caged-up, sorry-looking mutt that intrigued him.

The human who claimed she owned the dog had a shrill voice and a face he didn't trust. She had treated his human badly. He didn't like that. And she'd called him old and sneaky. Of all the nerve! He could tell the dog wasn't happy to see her either, even though he trotted after her on the end of a leash.

He heard the key turn in the cottage door and jumped to the floor at the sound of footsteps. Lunch at last. Maybe he'd forgive her for staying away so long.

Maybe.

"There you are," Faith called, stepping into the living room.

Watson sat on the floor near the sofa, idly cleaning one black paw and not even looking in her direction.

"Lunch with Aunt Eileen lasted a bit longer than I expected. Sorry." She threw her anorak on the back of the chair and kicked off her shoes.

"And I'm getting the cold shoulder why?" she asked as the cat continued to ignore her. "It's only been a few hours."

Faith picked Watson up in her arms and carried him to the pantry. After setting him down, she scooped out an extra helping of his favorite kibble and mixed it with canned tuna.

With a resigned twitch of his whiskers, Watson settled himself over his dish and began to eat.

Faith put the kettle on, then returned to the living room and sat on the sofa, delighting in the sensations of home. She never thought she would be so charmed by a humble cottage on the edge of the opulent mansion grounds with its topiaries and Victorian garden. She had never dreamed such splendor would be her lot to enjoy.

The cottage had been completely redecorated before her arrival, and its rooms were bright and airy. The welcoming fireplace surrounded by built-in bookcases gave her no end of joy on a brisk evening. She loved the trees that filtered heaven's light through graceful branches, the green-gold meadow that brightened the rocky coast. And when she closed her eyes she could hear the soft shushing of waves on the beach. The sound never failed to soothe. At night, she could listen to the ocean through the open window of her cottage as the curtains moved in a graceful, moonlit dance. Here in this quaint stone cottage existed comfort, serenity, and a world of beauty waiting to be explored.

She'd received her undergraduate degrees in library science and history from the University of Maine on a full scholarship, but sometimes Faith pinched herself to be certain she was really the librarian at Castleton Manor. Though she hadn't been management's first choice, she had earned respect, at least from Wolfe and well-qualified staff members who had become her friends. With Marlene, however, it was hard to know where she stood.

From the get-go, Faith had met with mystery at the manor, but that hadn't been the end of the surprising and unusual events.

Each new group of guests seemed to usher in some secret story. As exciting as it was to ferret out the facts, she was hoping for a calm retreat in which they would celebrate poetry in peace and fraternity. Her first literary love was mysteries, but she had profound respect for poetry that lived and breathed in every tree and mountain and human soul. How empty the world would be without its imagery and scintillating syllables.

She thought of favorite lines, fragments like Alfred, Lord Tennyson's "Flower in the Crannied Wall" and the classic "The Lady of Shalott" that she had memorized in high school and whose syllables still sang in her heart, the final stanza a prayer.

Who is this? and what is here?
And in the lighted palace near
Died the sound of royal cheer;
And they cross'd themselves for fear,
All the knights at Camelot:
But Lancelot mused a little space;
He said, "She has a lovely face;
God in his mercy lend her grace,
The Lady of Shalott."

Rap! Rap! Rap!
Faith jumped at the sound of the lion's-head knocker banging against the front door and headed for the tiny foyer off the living room.

Watson scurried out of the kitchen to wrap himself around her legs.

"So, am I forgiven now?" she asked, nearly tripping over him. She threaded her way to the door, wondering who was visiting in the middle of the afternoon. *Maybe Brooke or one of the groundskeepers.* Her tea would have to wait but hopefully not too long.

"It's about time you got here. I've been trying to get ahold of you." Marlene stood with her hands on her hips. She wore a cerulean-blue pantsuit with a gold-and-blue striped scarf. Her blonde hair was in a neat, no-nonsense bun at the nape of her neck. Heaven forbid a wisp of hair should detach itself and soften her long face with its pointed nose.

"Oh, I'm sorry." Faith stepped back so Marlene could enter, painfully aware of her own rumpled appearance in jeans and a Hawarden University sweatshirt. Windblown hair and bare feet completed the picture. She swallowed. "I had to go to town to run some errands. Then Midge needed a ride to make a call at the kennels here." She fell silent, pondering the disapproval on Marlene's face. The library wasn't scheduled to be open until after dinner on this first day of the retreat. Why should she explain her free time activities?

"I know about that fiasco with Miss Smythe and her dog." Marlene glared at Watson who stood looking at the door as though waiting for a chance to spring through it to freedom. "She's allergic to cats, you know, and she's had to lie down all afternoon with a headache. I don't understand why you have to take that animal everywhere with you."

Faith held back a sharp retort. Marlene was no champion of pets, but she displayed a special dislike of cats. Faith appreciated Castleton Manor's accommodation of pets accompanying their guests, but she didn't take Watson with her everywhere she went, as Marlene accused. She took a deep breath. "I can't imagine what you mean by fiasco. We were simply accompanying Midge to the kennels, where she'd been summoned by our staff."

"Well, the two of you intimated that Miss Smythe hadn't been taking proper care of her dog, and she was quite incensed." Marlene narrowed her eyes. "Hardly the way we want our guests to be treated. And then that animal of yours goes diving right at the poor dog."

Faith was sure she heard a low rumbling sound from Watson, who spun around from his spot near the door and sat down warily. "I assure you that we were polite to Miss Smythe, though she hardly returned the favor. I don't know what she told you, but the truth is that her dog did appear to be neglected. As for Watson, he didn't dive at Carlo. He was making friends. We only wanted to help, and I'm sorry the lady misunderstood our intentions."

Marlene's demeanor softened slightly. She cleared her throat. "Be that as it may, our first consideration must be to our guests. Now, I made a special trip over here to request your presence at the welcome dinner."

Faith was well aware that Marlene seldom made requests. She made demands. She frowned, thinking about her plans for a relaxing supper in her cottage and some prep time for her lecture this evening, and opened her mouth to protest.

But Marlene rushed on before Faith could say anything. "Actually, Miss Smythe asked for you personally."

She asked for me? Faith was stunned. This morning Emilie had stormed off with the Newfoundland, her nose in the air. Did Emilie want to insult her further? To demand some kind of apology she had no right to?

"For whatever reason, Miss Smythe would like you to sit with her at dinner. Since our guests come first, I must ask that you comply. Six o'clock. Don't be late." With that, Marlene turned, walked out the cottage door, and marched down the stone pathway.

Too late Faith realized that Watson had scooted out the door too. "Watson! Come back!" she called as he scampered toward the woods at the rear of the cottage. "If you miss your supper, you'll have to wait until my library hours are over," she added quietly, knowing of course that the cat wouldn't hear her.

Faith arrived at the dining room at six on the dot. Being summoned in such a peremptory manner had done little to heighten her enthusiasm for a grand dinner. Still, she had dressed carefully in a maroon A-line dress with jacket and tried not to dwell on the whys and wherefores of prickly assistant managers. She had delayed too, because she'd hoped that Watson would come home before she had to lock the cottage and head for the mansion. But he hadn't shown up.

White tablecloths and crimson napkins graced the tables in the immense dining room with its high ceilings and alabaster columns. Tall silver candles glowed in elegant glass holders ringed by deep-red silk flowers. On each table, the face of a famous poet looked out from a silver-edged frame. Among them were Robert Burns, T. S. Eliot, Marianne Moore, Carl Sandburg, and Elizabeth Barrett Browning. One could sit at the table of a favorite. Her personal choice would be Gerard Manley Hopkins, but Miss Emilie Smythe would surely sit at the Emily Dickinson table.

Faith found the table bearing the likeness of the poet of Amherst and perused the faces of four women and one gentleman seating themselves amid a flurry of conversation. She sat down next to a twenty-something woman with walnut-brown hair brushed to cover a thin, acne-scarred face. Faith detected a strange scent, something like menthol. Perhaps it was a medication the young woman used for her acne or to treat a cold.

The sullen young woman had an air of immaturity about her as she spoke to the lady seated next to her. "Someone should put a stop to that woman's rumors. She has no right to defame the reputation of America's greatest poet." Then she fell silent, staring down at her hands.

The subject of her derision had to be Emilie Smythe, whose claims to kinship with Dickinson had circulated. But Emilie was not here to defend herself and most certainly would not be welcome at the table. Faith scanned the dining room but didn't locate her.

At the podium, microphone poised in her well-manicured hand, Marlene waited for each guest to find a chair. When everyone was seated, Marlene gave a short welcome speech. Then dinner got under way.

At fifteen past the hour, there was still no sign of Emilie Smythe.

Marlene glanced over at Faith's table several times, her frown deepening with each look. Faith picked at her salad and engaged in light conversation around the table as the entrées were served, certain Emilie would make a grand entrance at any moment. There were no further comments about Emilie from the disgruntled young woman.

Marlene glanced at her phone, then rose from her place and strode to a side exit, gesturing for Faith to follow.

Faith obeyed reluctantly. *What now? Did Marlene get her wires crossed, or did Emilie find something better to do than have dinner with the owner of the "sneaky old cat" that "bothered" her dog?*

Marlene was all business. "Miss Smythe is not feeling well enough to leave her room, but she's asking for you to stop in to see her." She gave no apology or commiseration, and she didn't seem to find the request presumptuous.

"I suppose I could if there's time between dinner and my duties at the library," Faith said reasonably.

"Not later. Now, please. You know that the comfort of our guests is the top priority here at Castleton."

"But—"

"She's in the Emily Dickinson Suite. I'm sure you won't keep Miss Smythe waiting." Marlene turned on her heel and went back into the dining room.

The Emily Dickinson Suite was one of eighteen guest bedrooms located on the second floor. Faith found it at the top of the cantilevered marble staircase that never failed to take her breath away. She dawdled, marveling over the thousand-pound chandelier suspended from the middle of the majestic staircase and wondering what censure she would suffer from the offended lady.

She rapped on the dark, polished door. Seconds ticked by. With everyone gone to dinner, an eerie stillness prevailed. The very dust motes seemed to pause in midair. "Miss Smythe," she called through the door, "it's Faith Newberry."

After half a minute passed, she called once more.

She heard a slight rustle from within, and then a wary voice responded, "Come in."

Faith slowly pushed the door open and peeked in. All the guest bedrooms in the manor were large and marvelously decorated with a fireplace flanked by built-in bookshelves and a private luxury bathroom. The Emily Dickinson Suite was no exception, though only small touches of color offset the white draperies and quilt, the dark oak bedstead, and the dove-gray couches.

Near a wide window Miss Smythe sat erect, clutching the arms of the chair, with a white fur throw folded across the lap of her white dress. Her black hair, caught in a low bun at the neckline of her dress, presented a startling contrast to the whiteness of her shoulders. She confirmed her caller's identity with a glance before returning her attention to the window. It was fully dark, and the mansion's lovely grounds were bathed in moonlight.

"You asked to see me?" Faith prompted, disturbed by the woman's silence. "I'm sorry you're not feeling well."

Emilie's chest swelled a little as though she had taken a deep breath and was holding it. "Thank you," she said, still staring out the window. She clasped and unclasped her hands in her lap on top of the beaded bag she had worn crosswise over her chest that morning. "Sit, please." Emilie indicated a chair across from her own, then looked at the door, which Faith had closed behind her.

Faith took the offered seat.

Emilie turned to her guest. "I'm sure you haven't come out of the goodness of your heart," she said in a tone reminiscent of her earlier surliness.

Faith could feel her temper rising. Was there no limit to this woman's insults? She opened her mouth without the faintest idea of what to say.

But Emilie's voice broke through, this time strangely different in tone. "Never mind. I know what you think. That I'm a crazy woman fixated on a Victorian poet. And like everyone else, you don't believe that I'm related to her." She directed her gaze to the window once more. "I'm tired. I'm tired of it all, and that's why I'm making you a present of this." With a slightly trembling hand she held the beaded bag out to an astonished Faith. "You said you admired my reticule."

"Pardon me?" But Faith had heard her clearly.

"You may judge its letters and documents on the merits of your scholarship, which I understand are considerable, and you may make your own determination. In any case, I relinquish this reticule with its contents. I do not wish to see it again."

Faith swallowed a lump the size of a peach. "Miss Smythe—Emilie—I couldn't possibly accept this."

A look of panic whisked through Emilie's dark eyes like a comet. She closed them and pressed her lips together, as though in deep concentration or pain. After a few seconds, she looked up. "But you must. Please . . . I can't do this anymore!"

Do what? Pretend she's someone she isn't? But why now after so long pressing her claims? What is behind the fear so clearly revealed in her eyes and manner?

"There is a letter signed by me that releases this bag and its contents to you. To Faith Newberry, librarian at Castleton Manor." She leaned forward, dropped the bag into Faith's lap, and withdrew her hand as though it were on fire. Something black and fearful lurked in her eyes.

Faith felt the weight of the bag and the heavier burden of the promise being extracted. "Why are you giving this to me?"

Gazing off into a faraway space only she could see, Emilie recited the well-known Dickinson lines:

My life closed twice before its close;
It yet remains to see
If Immortality unveil

A third event to me,
So huge, so hopeless to conceive
As these that twice befell.
Parting is all we know of heaven,
And all we need of hell.

With that, Emilie put her hands to her face and bent forward like a cloud folded in upon itself. "Leave me now," she said, her voice a harsh whisper.

4

"It's so lovely here in the morning," Brooke Milner said as she leaned back against the chair in Faith's cottage. Her gaze roamed the kitchen with its view of the woods and the dappled sunlight reflecting on the oak table. "No wonder you love this place."

Faith had been delighted when Brooke phoned to invite herself over for breakfast and say she was bringing a treat. They'd become fast friends since Faith's first day on the job, when Brooke had helped her navigate the opulent halls of the mansion.

Midge had stopped in before her early-morning check on Carlo. She sipped her Earl Grey tea with relish, hands wrapped around her mug. Her nails were a bright pink dotted with tiny paw prints.

A humorous glint lit Brooke's blue eyes. "Has Wolfe been over for coffee lately?"

Faith groaned. Brooke was a hopeless romantic and loved teasing her about the handsome owner of Castleton Manor. Like Midge, Brooke was convinced that Wolfe had been around a great deal more often since Faith had taken the job as librarian.

But he was away much of the time with a wide range of responsibilities. When Wolfe was in town, he resided on the private third floor of the manor. He also had a flat in Kent, where he stayed when traveling to England for business. *He's so out of my league*, she thought. It was hard to imagine that he would have any time for a librarian living in the former gardener's cottage on his vast estate.

Faith was glad for Watson's abrupt leap onto her knees, derailing the subject of Wolfe. The cat stretched his neck to peer at the contents of the table, sniffed delicately, then curled into a ball on her lap.

Faith reached for another strawberry cream cheese pastry, Brooke's creation for the first morning of the poetry retreat. Brooke had a degree from Le Cordon Bleu College of Culinary Arts in Boston and was lauded for her ability to create incredible themed dishes. Not that she often partook of her own rich pastries, as evidenced by her willowy figure. "How did you manage to get out of the kitchen so early?" Faith asked.

"I have my ways," Brooke said mischievously, twirling a lock of platinum-blonde hair around her left ear. "Besides, it's a small, elite crowd for the retreat, and most of my work is done before the guests arrive for breakfast."

"Too bad Eileen isn't here," Midge remarked as she refilled her cup. "Then the club would be complete."

"That would be wonderful, but I guess I'll have to settle for the two of you," Faith said, grinning. "Especially when you come bringing gifts." She popped the last bite of Brooke's pastry into her mouth and deliberately smacked her lips. "You, my creative sous-chef, are going to have the guests eating out of your hand—literally!"

"I wonder if my ingredients should rhyme," Brooke mused.

"Rhyme is only one element of a poem," Faith said. "And it's not even the most effective. Imagery and rhythm carry much more weight. Still, you could present poetry lovers with names of dishes that rhyme, like 'high-stakes pancakes' or 'renegade lemonade.'"

Midge rolled her eyes, and Brooke grinned.

"Marlene was clever to place those photos of framed poets on the dinner tables last night," Brooke said. "Where would you have chosen to sit if you'd been there?"

"I *was* there. For a while anyway," Faith admitted. She hesitated, unwilling to talk about the whole business with Emilie Smythe until she'd had time to digest it.

When Emilie had dismissed her, Faith had not returned to the dining room. Puzzled and greatly uncomfortable, she'd gone back to her cottage to drop off the beaded bag and its dubious contents.

Then, after delivering her lecture on National Poetry Month, Faith was too tired to think about Emilie and her "gift," so she'd placed the bag behind a loose brick in the fireplace where she occasionally hid valuable items.

Brooke looked at Faith over the rim of her coffee cup. "Why were you there?"

"Command performance, à la the clever Marlene. I was supposed to sit at the Emily Dickinson table with one of the guests, but she never showed."

"Let me guess," Midge drawled. "The formidable Miss Emilie Faye Smythe?"

Faith nodded, but before she could comment further, Brooke broke in. "Oh, wasn't Emily Dickinson the one who stayed cooped up in her father's house and walked around wearing only white dresses all the time?"

Faith smiled. "That's been rumored and not without some degree of confirmation, but Dickinson is regarded as one of the most successful American poets of the nineteenth century. She wrote about large subjects through close observation of small, everyday details."

"I remember some poetry by this really popular guy—Rod somebody. When I was in high school, I had an English teacher who loved to recite his stuff. I even remember one of the poems because I wrote it in my notebook and carried it with me from freshman year to graduation." Brooke closed her eyes and recited:

It happens just because we need
to want and to be wanted too,
when love is here or gone
to lie down in the darkness
and listen to the warm.

"Rod McKuen," Faith supplied. He would be Brooke's kind of

writer, though many would not classify him as a serious poet. Fair or not, one critic had claimed that the masses ate McKuen up with a spoon while highbrow literary critics roasted him on a spit. Faith wasn't about to stain Brooke's memory of the songwriter and poet, so she didn't say anything else.

"When my boyfriend dumped me a week before the senior prom, I consoled myself by going to the library and reading every poem in his book," Brooke said wistfully. "The book was called *Listen to the Warm*. Isn't that delicious?"

Faith and Midge exchanged an indulgent look. They both loved sensitive, sweet-tempered Brooke, who invariably voted for a romance as the Candle House Book Club's next read.

Brooke sighed. "When that rich guy who owns an antique shop told me he never liked McKuen, it should have been a sign," she said resignedly. "Diva and Bling tried to warn me. Whenever he called they swam like they were being chased by a shark from one end of the tank to the other. I finally told the guy not to bother calling me anymore."

Diva and Bling were Brooke's angelfish. She treated them like family and bought every accoutrement ever marketed for their aquarium. Brooke was certain that her pets were in tune with her emotions and could give her signals relating to her active dating life.

"Well, there are plenty more fish in the sea," Midge quipped.

Faith raised an eyebrow at Midge and turned to Brooke. "I have an idea. Midge has business at the kennels. Why don't we go along? We could take the shore route. I won't be needed at the library until later, and it's such a beautiful day."

"I have a little more time before I need to get back to the manor. Okay with you?" Brooke asked Midge.

"Sure. You can protect me from the mistress of that big Newfie I've been treating." Midge made a face as she reached for her black vet's bag.

The subject of Brooke's latest romance and the instincts of the animal world were effectively tabled as they left the cottage for the impromptu outing. Watson seemed to know what they were planning because he had jumped from Faith's lap and raced to the door ahead of them, his stub of a tail bobbing with anticipation.

Faith turned up the collar of her jacket and breathed in the brisk spring air. She took the middle spot between Midge and Brooke, enjoying the company of her good friends. The sun warmed their faces as they trekked across the grounds. In the carefully tended topiary garden, Faith admired the leafy sculpture of two little girls reading and holding an umbrella over their heads.

The silvery ocean came into view through a thin band of trees as they traveled the sloping path down to the ocean. Waves, urged by a gentle wind, splashed against the rocks along the manor's private beach.

Faith remembered a little cove she had discovered. "I want to show you a place I found at the far end of the beach. It's right below that rocky reef and not too much of a detour off the shore road. Getting there is a bit tricky, but if you watch your step, it should be fine. And I promise the view is spectacular."

"We're with you," Brooke said. "So, what's this about a Newfie? Is there really one of those huge animals here?"

"A sweet old fellow called Carlo," Midge replied. "Just needs some attention for simple mange and a little TLC."

"He belongs to Emilie," Faith said, shivering slightly. Something about the eccentric woman unnerved her. "She didn't take kindly to Midge's reprimands."

"Hopefully a night's rest has improved her humor," Midge said.

Suddenly, they heard footsteps on the uphill path from the beach. Some other hardy individual had decided to walk along the ocean on this chilly spring morning, though it was early for guests to be up and about. A man came toward them and stopped abruptly, perhaps as surprised as they were to find he wasn't alone. He quickly resumed his pace, ambling toward them on long corduroy-clad legs, his windbreaker flapping over a tweed vest.

"That's Devon Hamlin," Brooke whispered to Faith as the man crested the hill. "The antique dealer I was just telling you about."

"Ladies," Hamlin acknowledged, touching the bill of his cap. "Fine morning." He gave Brooke a smile that didn't quite reach his eyes.

The man's appearance was striking, with prominent cheekbones, protruding ears, and a fringe of red hair ringing his forehead beneath a tweed cap. Colorless eyes almost disappeared into deep sockets beneath heavy auburn brows. Faith restrained the urge to stare. When he was out of earshot, she gave Brooke an inquiring look.

"He owns Hamlin's Antiques in town," she said breezily. "He purchased an ugly gold figurine my great-aunt left me. Gave me a good price too." She pursed her lips. "We dated a couple of times, but Diva and Bling just didn't warm up to him."

Faith smiled and raised an eyebrow. "He certainly has a face you wouldn't soon forget." She hadn't seen him at the welcome dinner, but she hadn't hung around long enough to meet the guests except for those at her table. As her thoughts turned to the previous night, she tamped down the discomfort of her encounter with Emilie.

"Watch your step, Watson," she called as the cat took off down the narrow path toward the coast. He had been trotting along beside them for the most part, occasionally jaunting into the brush or chasing a curly leaf before circling back to them. He'd apparently wearied of their sauntering pace because now he disappeared down the slope.

The cat kicked up his heels like a spring lamb and propelled himself down the rocky ledge. Let the humans take the smooth path—he was

no scaredy-cat. He loved the fishy scent of the sea, and more often than not he'd find a tasty morsel washed up along the shore, despite the groundskeepers' conspiracy to clear them away before he could get to them. If he was lucky this morning he'd snatch up a treat before his human got down to the rocky inlet and said things like "Yuck! Don't eat that." It wasn't that he didn't get appetizing meals at home. But sometimes he wanted variety.

He smelled something decidedly not fishlike. He twitched his nose. It smelled like wet dog, a most disagreeable odor. And yet there was something familiar about it. He hopped down toward the protected spot where good things washed up. He'd get there before the humans found him.

That was when he spotted the big mangy dog, who instead of chasing him like some wild maniac as most dogs did, had acted in quite a civilized—one might almost say friendly—manner. Maybe they could play another game as they had when he'd snuck out of the cottage yesterday. That would be fun.

The dog was making a low, mournful sound, his hindquarters half in the water with something white and filmy at his feet.

The cat prowled forward, wary, the canine's scent growing stronger in his nostrils. He paced back and forth awhile, hoping for adventure. His paw touched something. He tried to bat the bright object to the dog but missed. Slippery little thing! He sat back on his haunches and poked it with his paw. The thing bit him. He tried to flick it away with his sandpapery tongue, but it stuck there.

And then he heard his name. The humans were coming.

"Hey, that looks like Carlo." Faith pointed to the rocky end of the private beach, shielding her eyes from a rapidly brightening sun.

"What's he doing way down there?" Midge ran ahead with Brooke following.

Faith caught a glimpse of something in the water beside Carlo and froze as though an ominous hand had clutched her. She heard the startled cries of Midge and Brooke from what seemed like a long distance away. She hurried to the small sheltered inlet where a drenched Carlo rose unsteadily. But he made no attempt to shake the water from his fur.

Emilie Smythe lay wedged between two rocky outcroppings, her hair loose and trailing like black seaweed. The white cotton dress clung to her thin frame, its full skirt billowing from little rivulets of water swirling into the inlet's cavity and receding into the ocean. Her cape flapped open, hanging from one shoulder in a kind of romantic dance move. Her high-heeled boots, precisely laced, appeared undisturbed by whatever trauma she'd endured.

"Oh no. It can't be," Faith croaked. Instinctively, she caught Watson in her arms and forced herself to look down at the pale face, the severe features that had softened now, rendering them almost beautiful. Dark lashes swept the marble-like cheek and closed eyes.

Some distant echo came winging mournfully through Faith's mind as though Alfred, Lord Tennyson were singing in her ear.

> *For ere she reach'd upon the tide*
> *The first house by the water-side,*
> *Singing in her song she died,*
> *The Lady of Shalott.*

Midge knelt on the rock, speaking softly to Carlo and nudging him away from the body.

Next to Faith, Brooke stood still as a statue, her voice a frightened whisper. "Who is that?"

Faith recalled the despair on Emilie's face the night before when she had thrust the beaded bag into her lap. The frenzied words replayed themselves: *I'm tired. I'm tired of it all. Please . . . I can't do this anymore!*

Had Emilie been so distressed that she'd simply walked into the water?

Brooke's cold hand gripped her shoulder. "Who is she?" she demanded again.

Midge held her fingers against Emilie's neck. She cast a look of profound regret at her friends poised on the rock above her.

Faith swallowed against the enormous lump in her throat, the pounding of blood in her ears. "It's Emilie Smythe. And she's . . . dead."

5

"You three find the body?" Officer Bryan Laddy adjusted his glasses, then looked at Faith. He and Officer Mick Tobin had responded to their 911 call and were in the midst of their on-scene inspection.

The newest member of the police force, Bryan Laddy was in his twenties with hazel eyes and a well-toned physique that would give any woman pause. Faith knew he operated by the book and allowed nothing to intimidate him. But at the moment she would have preferred the calm intelligence and kind manner of Chief Andy Garris, who no doubt would want to talk to her soon.

Faith stood next to Brooke, watching the EMTs carry Emilie away. Nearby Midge comforted Carlo as Officer Tobin held the dog firmly. Tobin had been a wrestler in college and was still a force to be reckoned with in his early thirties. The ambulance rumbled off without a siren blaring.

No need to hurry now. Emilie Smythe is beyond help. Faith felt wooden and empty. Watson wriggled in her arms, but she held him tighter. Something was stuck in his fur just below his stubby tail. Her fingers closed over a bright green fishing lure. She pulled it off and absently dropped it into her jacket pocket, gaze riveted on the place where Emilie had been.

How could this be happening? Hadn't she just talked with Emilie in the lovely Dickinson room? She recalled the trembling of Emilie's hand and her doleful eyes as she held out the beaded bag to her.

"Miss Newberry?" Laddy prodded.

"Yes, we discovered the body. We were having breakfast together and decided to go with Midge to the kennels to check on the dog."

Faith drew in her breath as Carlo's whine deepened. "We took the shore road. It was such a beautiful day." *How can we speak of the inanities of weather in the same sentence with what has happened here?* "We detoured down to the bay and saw Carlo. It seemed odd for him to be out there."

Watson squirmed like mad, so she let him hop down. The cat headed straight for Carlo, then stopped a few feet away from him, twirled around, and sat down, facing the big dog, as though to determine what he was doing here.

"Is that Miss Smythe's dog?" Laddy asked.

Faith nodded. "His name is Carlo. We just met him yesterday at the kennels. Miss Smythe too. She is—that is, she *was* a guest at the poetry retreat. As you know, guests can bring their pets to Castleton Manor. Midge treated the dog for mange, and then I drove her back to town." She hesitated. There was no need to mention Emilie's disgruntled behavior over Carlo's treatment and the presence of Watson.

Officer Laddy stopped taking notes on his phone and peered at her over the top of his glasses. "You seem to have a knack for discovering bodies."

Faith grimaced and clasped her hands together to steady herself. She did have a history with the Lighthouse Bay Police Department. When she'd first taken the job of librarian at Castleton Manor, she'd discovered a murder victim. For a while Faith had even been a suspect, but in the end she and Watson had helped the police find the real culprit. It hadn't been the last time she'd helped solve such a crime.

But this time it wasn't murder. Was it?

"How long has she been here?" Brooke asked the officer.

"Can't be sure yet, but I'd say probably four or five hours."

Faith checked her watch. It was now a little past eight thirty. She and Brooke and Midge had met at the cottage at seven so as not to infringe on their workday. That meant Emilie might have been here at three or four in the morning. In the dark, cold strivings before dawn. With the icy waves whispering over her. She shivered at the thought.

"We'll know more later." Laddy tapped his phone. "After Greco's report comes in."

A vision of the short, balding Dr. Greco flashed through Faith's mind. She imagined the coroner, intent on solving the riddle of death, and a new shiver ran through her. Hoping for reassurance, she glanced in Midge's direction.

"If y'all don't mind, I'd like to take Carlo back to the kennels," Midge said in her most polite Southern accent. "Poor boy, he's obviously upset." She regarded the canine, who was still being restrained by Officer Tobin.

"Is the dog dangerous?" Laddy asked, folding his arms across his chest. "Maybe he knocked her over and . . ." He shrugged and left his sentence unfinished.

"That sweet old fellow?" Midge interjected. "He's as gentle as a lamb."

"Maybe a lamb with a powerful karate chop," Tobin remarked with a grin. He liked to make jokes, but Faith had learned that he was an able defender of the peace. He brushed his free hand through his thick blond hair. "He's mighty eager to chase that ambulance. That's for sure."

"The Newfoundland is a protective and courageous breed. Carlo was most likely trying to protect his mistress. Though she didn't take very good care of him in my view," Midge confessed, blushing slightly.

Faith studied the rocky ledge above the inlet. The spot was beyond the beach area and only seven or eight feet down to the water. Still, to lose one's footing there could be treacherous. Guests to the manor were frequently warned to stay within the safe confines of the beach.

"Well, something made her go over the ledge. You see anyone in the area?" Laddy looked from one to the other, his gaze finally settling on Faith.

She caught Brooke's eye, suddenly remembering Devon Hamlin coming along the shore road, coat flapping, ears like propellers in the wind. "We did see someone. Another guest at the manor, but he—" Faith stopped as the possibility that someone could have caused Emilie's death flashed through her mind once again.

"Devon Hamlin. Of Hamlin's Antiques in town," Brooke offered softly.

"When was this?" Laddy asked. Faith could almost see the antennae rising above his dark head.

"Not more than ten minutes or so before we crested the hill above the beach. We stopped to talk briefly, but he didn't seem upset or anything." *Did he see Emilie—either alive or dead? Had he also detoured past the beach onto the rocky overlook, perhaps curious to see the view? Or did he . . . ?* But that didn't make any sense. If Devon had seen Emilie lying there, he would have said something. And if he had done something to her, he wouldn't hang around for four or five hours and wait to be discovered.

"We'll want to speak with him. And with anyone who knew or had occasion to talk to the victim." Laddy paused, considering. "Mr. Jaxon, of course, if he's in the country, or whoever's in charge." He waved Midge off as she headed to the kennels with a nervous Carlo. He turned to Faith and Brooke. "I'll give you two a lift back."

Faith's heart sank. Marlene wasn't going to be happy about another mystery brewing. Something to set her guests on edge, to sully the image of Castleton Manor.

But a woman was dead. What could be more important than that?

As they rode up the winding drive, Faith could see Marlene and some other guests and staff outside the manor. A few curious onlookers stood on the loggia, watching. They couldn't have missed the scream of the ambulance on its way to the beach. Perhaps they'd witnessed the vehicle crawl back silently the way it had come.

Marlene rocked forward as though to hasten the progress of the police car heading her way. She was perfectly turned out in a powder-blue suit and navy pumps. A scarf of royal blue and white stripes set off her blonde chignon.

Faith hurried toward Marlene with Brooke in tow and Officer Laddy several paces behind. "Maybe it would be best to go inside. To your office perhaps?" She glanced meaningfully at the watching guests.

"What on earth is going on? What are the police doing here?" Marlene demanded, ignoring Faith's suggestion entirely. Her eyes glittered in the sunlight beneath brows furrowed into one angry line.

Laddy caught up to them and nodded at Marlene, his glasses slipping down the bridge of his nose. "I'm afraid there's been an accident. One of the manor's guests."

Marlene's face turned chalk white, and she staggered back a step. "An accident? What? Who?"

Faith instinctively put out a hand to steady the assistant manager.

"Miss Emilie Smythe," Officer Laddy filled in. "Can you confirm that she's a registered guest at the manor?"

"Yes, of course she is," Marlene snapped. "Surely our librarian informed you." She looked at Faith coldly. "But what about Miss Smythe? Where is she?"

He appeared behind Marlene so quickly that Faith didn't even see his approach. So the rumors had been correct. Wolfe was back. He looked fit and tan, but vague shadows circled his eyes, and it seemed to Faith that his shoulders drooped slightly. The business of Jaxon enterprises frequently took him away, sometimes to far-flung places in Europe or even Asia. Maybe he'd taken a red-eye flight back to Massachusetts.

His eyes sought Faith's briefly, piercing her with what might have been either consternation or concern, and she felt a lurch somewhere between her heart and her stomach.

"Let's go inside, shall we?" Wolfe said in a tone that left no room for argument. "I believe your office will be suitable." He put a hand on Marlene's elbow and steered her to the door.

They moved quietly through the manor and went downstairs. The offices were located in the basement in what had once been the servants' quarters.

Wolfe stopped at the door marked *Assistant Manager* and ushered them inside. He extended his arm to indicate the round table in the center of Marlene's spacious office.

The little group filled five of the six walnut chairs upholstered in pale blue leather.

"Ms. Russell is in charge when I'm away," Wolfe explained to Officer Laddy. "I've just returned today, but I'm sure she can provide any information you may need."

"Now what's this about Miss Smythe?" Marlene asked. "She's booked into the Emily Dickinson Suite, and she's attending our poetry retreat."

Faith caught Brooke's eye, then lowered her head, feeling profoundly sad. *Not anymore.*

"I'm sorry to tell you that Miss Smythe was found unresponsive on the beach this morning," Officer Laddy said. "She was declared dead at the scene."

For a few seconds the silence in the office was palpable.

"What happened?" Wolfe asked, breaking the silence.

"We believe she fell from that rocky overlook at the far end of your private beach very early this morning," Laddy said. "She may have hit her head and then drowned." He nodded to Faith and Brooke. "Your employees here found her and her dog. Carlo, isn't it? The vet who was also there took him back to the kennels."

"But last night she was . . . I talked with her—" Marlene sought Wolfe's gaze as if for help or comfort. Then she turned to Faith, leaned forward in her chair, and pointed at her. "You saw her last night. She wasn't feeling well and couldn't come to dinner. She had a headache or something, probably because of that cat of yours pestering her dog."

"Watson was with us at the kennels, but he wasn't causing any trouble," Faith pointed out.

Marlene went on in her accusatory tone as if she hadn't even heard Faith. "She asked you to come to her room. What did she say to you?"

Faith had not told anyone about Emilie's "gift"—the bag containing documents that supposedly proved she was the great-great-granddaughter of the famous poet. She'd simply tucked it into her favorite hiding place in her cottage and gone on to deliver her lecture on National Poetry Month. She had forgotten about it until just now. She briefly relayed the gist of what had transpired.

"But she's been bragging about having proof of her relation to Emily Dickinson for years," Marlene said. "Why would she suddenly give it up? And why to you?"

The inference was clearly insulting, but Faith swallowed the hurt. "I suppose Emilie thought I would know how to investigate her claims because I'm a librarian." She paused, considering whether to tell them more. She decided to continue. "Emilie said she was tired of it all. Those were her words. 'I'm tired of it all. I can't do this anymore.' She was very distressed." Faith shuddered, recalling the depression that had clouded the room.

Faith noticed Wolfe staring down at his folded hands. Was he perhaps embarrassed by his prickly assistant manager or considering the somber possibility that someone had deliberately taken her own life at Castleton Manor? She went on, more softly this time. "She told me to decide about her identity on the merits of my scholarship. She gave the documents to me and said she didn't want to see them again."

"That's the most bizarre thing I've ever heard," Marlene protested. "Everyone knew she was on the loony side. Brilliant in many ways, of course, but not all there." She surveyed Faith. "You might be the last person to have seen her alive."

Brooke, who had been completely silent during this impromptu meeting, broke in. "Someone at the kennels must have seen Emilie when she went to get Carlo out. Or one of the staff who turned her bed down or brought her room service."

"At this point, we have more questions than answers," Officer Laddy said, rising. "We'll be investigating Miss Smythe's death, but the important thing now is to notify the woman's next of kin." He looked pointedly at Marlene. Clearly, he was waiting for names and addresses.

Next to Laddy, Wolfe got up and cleared his throat. "Bentley Smythe." He pressed his lips together briefly, then added, "The lady's brother and guardian. He lives on Martha's Vineyard and owns the Williamson Estate. He's a big dealer in imported goods and travels frequently. Perhaps I should be the one to inform him of his sister's death since it happened here at Castleton."

Officer Laddy hesitated, as though considering proper procedure. "Well, I see no problem with that." He tucked his phone into his jacket pocket. "We'll need him to identify the body."

"There's a half sister as well," Wolfe stated. "Margaret owns the bait and tackle shop just outside the limits of Lighthouse Bay. She lives right next to the pier."

"Maggie Haggedorn?" Laddy asked, pushing his glasses up with interest.

Wolfe nodded, his features unreadable.

Faith felt her pulse pick up, remembering Aunt Eileen's description. *The black sheep of the Smythe dynasty. She owns a bait and tackle shop and has a chip on her shoulder the size of Manhattan.*

What would the passing of her wealthy half sister mean to Maggie Haggedorn? To the brother who was Emilie's guardian according to Wolfe?

And more than all these questions, what had happened out there in the dark April morning?

6

The day after the tragic discovery on the beach, Faith was glad to stay close to the library. It was her job, of course, and she was expected to be available to the poetry retreat guests. Fortunately, the spectacular surroundings of the library with its glowing fireplace and comfortable red velvet furniture had become like home. The thousands of volumes in the two-story built-in bookcases were like friends waiting to soothe the anxieties and foreboding of the previous day.

She glanced at the locked glass cases containing some of the library's rare books, including several volumes of poetry collections. These and other books had been perused by the retreat attendees coming and going throughout the morning.

Some of the guests were merely curious about the death of Emilie Smythe, and Faith had deflected many of their comments and questions. Others searched for a particular volume of poetry among the vast collection of works by T. S. Eliot, Wilfred Owen, Charles Bukowski, Robert Frost, and other famous names. Works by poets such as Robert Burns, William Blake, and William Wordsworth were popular choices too, as were Shakespeare and the two Johns—Milton and Donne.

Now, with guests lingering in the banquet hall following lunch or resting in their suites, it was quiet in the library. Faith sat at her desk, an antique wonder that still amazed her. Its legs were made of intricately carved walnut, and its sides were decorated with relief carving that resembled a large cameo, featuring the face of some distant Jaxon family ancestor. At first, she had been too awed by the antique desk for comfort, but she had made it her own with personal pens and pencils, some engraved with her name, and a paperweight her father had given her containing a sepia replica of her grandmother's face.

"And I must say, Rumpy, having you here makes it all perfect." She scratched behind Watson's silken ears as the cat lay curled in her lap.

He stopped purring and stretched a hind leg to show his disapproval at the mention of the nickname.

Faith occasionally called him Rumpy because of the accidental loss of most of his tail, which had left behind a little stump. The loss didn't impede his movements much, but whenever he was called Rumpy, he completely ignored the caller, except perhaps when it came to dinner.

Faith grinned, recalling Ernest Hemingway's insight: "A cat has absolute emotional honesty: human beings, for one reason or another, may hide their feelings, but a cat does not."

Watson's irritation was short-lived, and soon he relaxed and began purring again.

As she smoothed the sleek, black fur from his head to his stumpy tail, she remembered another observation, this one by Albert Schweitzer: "There are two means of refuge from the miseries of life: music and cats."

It was a rare pleasure to be allowed to bring Watson with her to work. A few visitors to the library had also brought pets with them this morning. *The Jaxon family has made Castleton Manor unique among grand mansions, and I'm fortunate to have landed a position here.*

At least she'd thought so until yesterday. Emilie's tragic death left everyone shocked and apprehensive. It was a stroke of luck that the guests were already scheduled to attend a local production of a play that evening. After the awful events of the day, they seemed to enjoy *Much Ado About Nothing*. Faith had gone along at Marlene's insistence and tried to immerse herself in the play involving two sets of lovers, but it was impossible to erase the memory of Emilie's body in the little inlet at the base of the rocky ledge.

At two o'clock she got up from her desk and was about to lock the library door when a man came in. Watson took the opportunity to exit, causing the visitor to move back to avoid stepping on him. The tall man, who looked to be in his forties, recovered quickly and proceeded into the library, tucking black gloves into his pocket, then loosening a soft wool scarf. His appearance was impressive, even though he had coupled his expensive gray Italian suit with every man's favorite off-duty button-down: the chambray shirt. The combination struck just the right look of elegance and comfort. A short, well-trimmed beard complemented the oval of his face—a face that seemed oddly familiar but strange at the same time.

He scanned the library confines and located Faith, then strode toward her with the grace of a man in command of social situations, one hand loosely in the pocket of his trousers. Everything about him shouted wealth and position. "Are you Miss Newberry?" he asked. He didn't smile but engaged her focus directly.

She felt suddenly at a loss for words. "Y-yes," she stammered, "I'm Faith Newberry. The librarian here at the manor." She put out her hand, which he did not take.

Instead, he bowed. "Bentley Smythe," he said in a resonant voice. "Wolfe told me where to find you."

Disturbingly inquisitive eyes the color of burnished walnut bored into her. His hair was dark. Not as deeply black as Emilie's but close enough that Faith realized why he seemed familiar. "Oh," she said softly, "I am so very sorry for your—"

"I hope this isn't a bad time," he interrupted before she could complete her sentence.

"No. I was just closing up." Something in Bentley's piercing stare was both troubling and compelling. Faith wanted to look away but couldn't. *What does one say in the presence of another's grief?* She'd always contended that most people said far too much.

He continued to gaze at her intently, and when his shoulders drooped, she asked tentatively, "Are you all right?" *Stupid question. How would this man be all right when he's just learned his sister is dead?*

"Yes, yes." Bentley ran a hand across his beard, as though impatient. All at once, he appeared overcome.

"Please sit down," Faith offered, motioning to the nearest chair.

He staggered over to it, and Faith took the chair across from him. They were both silent for a few seconds.

"I'm so sorry about Miss—I mean, Emilie." Faith wanted to say something more, tell him she understood how hard it was to lose a family member. She'd been distraught when her beloved grandmother had passed away. Finding Watson when she'd felt so lost and alone had helped her to move on.

Bentley sighed. "I'm afraid my sister has been troubled for some time. Actually, she's needed special looking after since she was a child," he admitted, absently touching the band of his gold watch.

He's assuming his sister killed herself, Faith realized in surprise. *That she jumped off the cliff of her own volition.* But the cause of death hadn't been officially determined. *Why doesn't he consider that she might have fallen accidentally or that someone—?* She stopped her thoughts, not wanting to even imagine foul play. And yet it was possible. Wouldn't Bentley Smythe want to know for sure?

"Did you know my sister?" he asked, bringing her out of her thoughts. A curious glint lightened his dark eyes, giving them an amber cast. He had regained his control and sat up straight in the chair.

"Not very well, I'm sorry to say," Faith replied, unnerved by his directness, his stunning good looks. "I only met her the other day here at the poetry retreat."

"But doubtless you've heard about her." Bentley paused, as though trying to express his thoughts. "She was fixated on the famous poet who had a connection to our family. Indeed, we are descended from the Edward Smythe who mentored Emily Dickinson, but my sister believed—or wanted to believe—that the relationship involved more than that. The experts aren't convinced." A humorous gleam whisked through his eyes. "Of course, she could be right. No one knows for sure."

Faith felt uncomfortable talking about the woman who could

no longer defend herself or her beliefs. Did Bentley subscribe to the possibility? What did he think about the so-called documents she'd carried in her beaded bag? Had he encouraged Emilie in her struggle to prove the relationship that was flatly debunked by the experts, or had he merely humored her? Faith searched the man's face. What could she who knew so little about Emilie offer this man bereaved of his sister? And why had he sought her out?

As though he'd discerned her questions, Bentley said in a more serious tone, "I understand you were the one who found my sister."

"Yes, my two friends and I. While we were walking along the beach, my cat took off toward the rocks. We followed him to bring him back and that was when—"

"That was your cat that almost knocked me over when I was coming in?"

She nodded.

"Animals in the Jaxon mansion!" Bentley grinned. "The family always was a bit eccentric."

Was he laughing at them? Or simply expressing some comic relief in dire circumstances? Faith felt compelled to defend her employer. "It works very well. Every accommodation is made to ensure the hygiene and comfort of all the guests, whether they have pets or not. And the animals are well cared for, I can assure you."

"I didn't mean to criticize." He cocked his head almost flirtatiously. "Wolfe would be pleased to know how loyal his employees are."

She looked away from Bentley's intrusive stare, unsure how to respond. Did he hope to deflect his grief with these comments? Or was he less broken up over Emilie's demise than one might expect him to be? "Is there something I can do for you?" Faith inquired.

And suddenly his demeanor changed. Bentley bowed his head as though contrite and fidgeted with his slender, sun-browned hands. "Forgive me." He shook his head slowly, the light turning his dark hair nearly copper. "She used to love walking along the beach, searching for shells and dragging them home. She'd fill the house with them. It drove us all crazy."

Faith tried to imagine the proud, uptight woman caressing a seashell in loving hands. What had stolen that early joy?

"I guess I just wanted to talk to someone who was with her when she . . . before she . . ." He met her eyes, once again compelling her gaze.

What could she say? She had met a disgruntled Emilie briefly at Castleton's kennels and shared a conversation that was anything but informative or warm. As for the bag and its alleged contents, which she had yet to peruse, should she offer them to Bentley? After all, he was Emilie's brother. Did he, as her guardian, have the right to them? And what about the half sister, Maggie Haggedorn?

She struggled to find something to say that would satisfy him or bring comfort. "I'm really sorry, Mr. Smythe."

"Please call me Bentley."

But she couldn't form the name on her tongue, so she moved on. "When my friends and I came upon your sister, she was already—" She stopped, not wanting to give expression to the shocking, inert state in which she had found Emilie. "She was alone, except for Carlo."

A shadow passed over his eyes.

"Her dog, a very large Newfoundland," Faith said. She knew she was rambling, but she didn't know what to say. "He was watching over her. He's so gentle and sweet. Watson—that's my cat—is quite mesmerized by him."

"I see." He drew a hand across his jaw thoughtfully.

She recalled the startling image—the huge Newfie guarding his mistress, keeping her from drifting back into the water. Had he pulled her to shore? Had he dragged her up to the sandy inlet? Such faithfulness, despite Emilie's apparent carelessness where the animal was concerned. Yet Officer Laddy had suggested that Carlo might have knocked her into the water in the first place. Faith couldn't believe it. But what had those soulful brown eyes seen? What had happened to Emilie?

Bentley studied Faith as though he could read something inside her, then dropped his hands into his pockets. "I have been out of the country, and I left Emilie in the care of our housekeeper, a fine woman. Emilie must have adopted the animal while I was away." He raised an eyebrow. "Carlo. That's the name—"

"Yes, the name of the famous poet's dog."

"That's just like Emilie." Bentley frowned, pursing his lips. "Something must be done for the animal, of course. Perhaps he can remain here for now. Wolfe has been kind enough to offer me sanctuary at Castleton Manor until—well, until arrangements can be made. That way I'll be available when needed."

They were silent for a moment, and Faith wondered what else to say.

Bentley rose and took a step toward her. "I've been terribly selfish. You were on your way out, and I have monopolized your time." He gave another little bow and extended a hand. "Allow me to escort you to your lodging or wherever you're off to."

Faith stood, then collected her purse and adjusted the strap over her shoulder. "There's no need. My cottage isn't far."

"Please. You've been very kind." Bentley walked with her to the door.

She was aware of how little space there was between them as they moved across the elegant foyer and out into the brisk afternoon.

"I must say, Wolfe has done quite well for himself," he remarked, scanning the magnificent manor and grounds. "Biltmore has nothing over this fabulous place."

"He's made good on his family heritage but not just for himself," Faith said, surprising herself at her compulsion to speak up for Wolfe. "He's welcomed hundreds of guests here to enjoy the manor and all its amenities, including the library with its vast collection of books. I feel honored to work here, really honored."

Bentley gave her a sidelong glance. "As I said, Wolfe is fortunate to have such a loyal staff." He strode easily beside her, his arm occasionally brushing hers.

"Have you known him long?" she asked, unsettled by his closeness.

"Wolfe and I were friends in college," he answered. "We once went on a safari together."

"Oh, you like to hunt?"

Bentley nodded, then peered into the distance. "In fact, I used to own a hunting cabin not far from here."

After a few moments of silence, Faith changed the subject. "I was wondering how your other sister is taking the news."

"Half sister," Bentley corrected sharply, then took a deep breath and slowly exhaled. "Maggie is our half sister. A year or so after Maggie's mother died, Father married my mother. I'm afraid Maggie never accepted her new mother or Emilie and me when we came along. After Maggie left home she had no use for any of us, especially after Father died."

Faith swallowed. She recalled Aunt Eileen's description of Maggie as a recluse with a chip on her shoulder. Odd. A woman in her fifties living alone and keeping a bait and tackle shop while her half siblings lived in an opulent estate. "But she's still a member of your family."

"Yes," he said and brushed a hand over his beard. "I advised her of Emilie's death, but she's left the details to me. She refused to go with me to identify the body."

"I'm so sorry," Faith whispered.

"Thanks," he said shortly, "but we're used to it. She's chosen her life, and it doesn't include me. Well, that's what we all do, isn't it? Make our choices?"

It sounded so cavalier. A defense mechanism perhaps. Some men found it difficult to communicate on an emotional level.

Faith was glad they were almost at her cottage. She longed to shut out the world with its messy problems, to enjoy the simple pleasures of a comfortable house, a cup of fragrant tea, and the welcoming presence of her cat.

And when she looked up, there he was as if summoned by her thoughts, sitting on the back of the couch and watching their approach through the window. Watson didn't move when they drew closer, didn't hop down to meet her at the door as he often did. He simply peered at them through narrowed eyes.

"You have a welcoming committee," Bentley said with a smile.

"Pets can be very comforting," she said.

"Yes, well, they can also cramp your style. My work keeps me on the go too much to be bothered with caring for a domesticated animal, and pets are not allowed in most places where I travel. Not like they are here at Castleton Manor." A disparaging smirk turned the corner of his mouth down.

So much for hoping for a good home for Carlo, she thought. Bentley Smythe wasn't about to adopt him. Of course, who could blame him?

They had stopped at her door, but he seemed disinclined to end their conversation, so they stood in uncomfortable silence.

"Well, it was good to meet you, Mr. Smythe."

"Bentley," he reminded her. "And it was good to meet you. I was hoping we might have an opportunity to talk once more since I won't be leaving right away."

Faith had told him what she knew about his sister, which was paltry at best. Really, she had nothing else to say. *What more does he expect?*

He was watching her, those deep eyes searching for something, wanting something. What? A magnetic quality in their depths drew her.

She shrugged, hoping to appear unaffected, and struggled to tamp down her embarrassment. "I'm in the library most days. Once again, I'm sorry about Emilie. And I'm sorry I couldn't be more help." She rushed inside before he could say anything else, but she was aware of a look of perplexity or possibly defeat on his handsome face.

Way to go, she reproached herself as she closed the cottage door. *A rich, handsome man shows that he likes me and wants to see me again, and I brush him off.*

Watson, unaffected by her self-censure, jumped down from the sofa in one quick movement and wrapped himself around her feet.

7

"How are you, dear?" Aunt Eileen's voice trilled warm and lilting through the phone.

"To tell the truth, I've been better," Faith said, shifting the phone to her left ear. She might say she was fine to some people, but when Aunt Eileen asked that question, she genuinely wanted to know. And something in the voice so like her mother's broke through any reserve she'd hoped to cultivate and made her throat ache. "Things have been pretty chaotic around here."

"I heard about poor Emilie Smythe drowning. Do they know how it happened?"

"No, the investigation and autopsy haven't been completed yet." She fought against the tears that threatened. "Midge and Brooke and I were the ones who found her and called for help. She was in the water just below the rocky ledge at the end of the beach. Her dog, Carlo, was standing over her."

"Oh no!" Eileen sounded astonished. "I'm so sorry."

"It happened yesterday morning," Faith said, drawing herself up in the chair by the window. She must keep calm if at all possible. "We were questioned by the police, and there's been a flood of inquiries and gossip. Marlene was fit to be tied, which is nothing new, I know, but this has really rattled her."

"I can imagine," Eileen said knowingly.

"At least Wolfe is back, and he's been able to smooth things over for the time being."

"I'm so glad. Wolfe is levelheaded and good with people. He'll know how to handle the situation."

"Yes," Faith said, picturing the brief exchange between them, a warm meeting of gazes, and the difference it had made after the experience of finding Emilie. A loyal friend could be a great comfort in turmoil. In the days since she'd arrived at the manor, she had come to appreciate his kindness and interest in her work.

And she had to admit she found herself thinking about him more than was probably good for her. She knew it was foolish. Wolfe was a sought-after bachelor who turned the head of every woman he met. Besides, she was in no hurry to get involved with someone. Heartache was a strong reminder not to make yourself vulnerable again.

"Are you sure you're all right?" Eileen asked, derailing Faith's thoughts. "I could come over."

"No thanks, but I do need your help—your expertise, actually. You see, Emilie gave me something before she died. It was so strange." Faith swallowed, glad for Watson's warm weight on her lap. He'd been coiled there since she'd gotten back to the cottage this afternoon. He seemed to know she needed his companionship. "Remember how you told me that she was always talking about Emily Dickinson and boasting about having proof that she was related to her?"

"Yes, most everyone around this area has heard about it. Poor girl, she needed to believe that the poet and her great-great-grandfather were lovers."

"Well, I couldn't have been more surprised when she gave me her beaded bag, which I had admired when we first met. She said it held the documents that proved her connection to Emily Dickinson, and she wanted me to have them. She told me she didn't want them anymore, that I could do whatever I wanted with them. She had this sort of wild look in her eyes, and she was terribly nervous."

Aunt Eileen remained quiet, and Faith continued. "I told her I couldn't accept them, but she said that I had to and pleaded with me to take them. I just didn't know what to make of it all, and then she dropped the bag on my lap and told me to leave her suite. I was extremely uncomfortable."

"What did you do?"

"I took the bag and got out of her room like she told me to," Faith responded. "I had a lecture to give in less than half an hour, so I returned to my cottage and put the bag behind the loose brick in my fireplace. I thought she would probably change her mind the next day and want it back. And frankly, the thing gave me the willies. I went to bed after my lecture and didn't touch the bag or look inside it." She felt a chill wash over her.

"Do you think she was planning to end her life?" Eileen's voice was small, as if she didn't want to ask.

"I don't know what to think. And that brings me to my request. I need to review the contents of Emilie's bag." Emilie's claims should be considered honestly and carefully. Faith owed her that much. "But I don't want to do it alone. I'd appreciate getting your take on it. I'm going to see if Midge and Brooke can come too. Do you have some time tomorrow?"

"Of course, honey. Come to Candle House."

"That would be great, if you're sure it's all right," Faith said, feeling better at the prospect of being with Eileen and her good friends in the beautiful old candle house that had been converted into a library. The four of them had weathered other storms together and even solved some mysteries along the way. They would work through this too. "The retreat members will be in poetry workshops all morning, so I don't have to be at the manor library until the afternoon."

"How about ten o'clock?" Eileen suggested. "I'll supply the refreshments for coffee break. I don't have Brooke's talent with gourmet desserts, but I'll come up with something palatable. I'm looking forward to seeing you, dear. Brooke and Midge too. And try not to worry too much."

"I knew I could count on you," Faith said. Aunt Eileen could always lift her spirits. "We'll be there. And thank you. Thank you so much."

After saying goodbye to Eileen, she looked down at her cat. "Well, it should be interesting, don't you think, Rumpy?"

Watson raised his head and gave her an imperious—if sleepy—gaze before recurling himself in the nest of her lap.

She smiled. *When a cat needs a nap, he'll put up with all manner of indignities*, she thought.

"And I promise we'll go see Carlo soon." She smoothed his silken fur and heard the rumble of his contented purr. She sighed. "What's to become of the big old Newfie now?" she whispered and leaned back in the plush chair that faced the fireplace. Even though it was April, there was still a chill in the air, and she wished she had lit a fire. Still, it was wonderful to be inside her peaceful cottage and away from the ambiguities of the world.

She knew she should go over her plans for the poetry reading that Marlene had ordered her to conduct in the library tomorrow night, but it felt good to snuggle with Watson on her lap and simply relax. She wasn't aware she was growing sleepy nor how long she had remained warm and cozy in her favorite chair when a light rap on the door woke her. She sprang up, sending Watson flying.

"Hello, Faith." Wolfe stood on the stone threshold, his silver-tinged dark hair tousled from the wind. A plaid scarf, his only protection from the brisk weather, was draped over the shoulders of his stylish suit. "I hope I haven't disturbed you."

"Oh no," she said, delighted and at the same time wishing she had known he was coming. Her blouse was askew, and her skirt had to be a mass of wrinkles. *I must look like something the cat dragged in.* Even though she didn't say it out loud, she glanced apologetically at Watson, who settled onto the back of the sofa to survey their company. With a quick brush of her hand, she smoothed her hair and ushered Wolfe inside.

"With all that's happened, this is the first opportunity I've had to see you," he said in a low, resonant voice. His smile transformed the tired look Faith had noted when he'd greeted Officer Laddy the day Emilie had died.

"Welcome back," Faith said. She'd forgotten how blue his eyes were—not the pedestrian, everyday sort of blue, but like stained glass rimmed with sunlight. "Everyone has missed you." She refrained from saying that she in particular had missed him. It wasn't something she wanted to admit even to herself.

"I wanted you to know how sorry I am about Miss Smythe. I mean, you finding her like that. It must have been really hard on you. On Brooke and Midge too." Wolfe looked down at his hands briefly. "I'm glad that you weren't alone this time."

Faith was glad too. When she'd encountered a victim shortly after arriving at the manor, she had been without the emotional support of her friends. It had been a daunting introduction to her new position and a time of tremendous uncertainty and upheaval. She had wanted to put as much distance as possible between herself and Lighthouse Bay.

"It was awful," she admitted. "It *is* awful. I wish we could have known she was suffering. I wish we could have done something." As she said it, Faith realized that even she concluded that Emilie had taken her own life. Had she so quickly bought into Bentley's explanation? To everyone else's suspicion? She allowed herself to gaze deeply into Wolfe's eyes. "This must be hard on you too, being her brother's friend."

Was it her imagination, or did a cloud pass over those amazing eyes?

"But where are my manners?" Faith said. "Please come in and sit down awhile." She heard the hopeful tone in her voice and struggled for a casual air. "Can I get you a cup of coffee or something? I also have some fudge brownies."

"An offer I can't refuse," Wolfe said with a tired smile as he followed her into the living room. "After the red-eye flight, then a less-than-welcome greeting when I got home, I'd enjoy a few minutes of calm." He glanced around the colorful room, at the green plants threading their way across the window cornice where a late-afternoon sun shone in. "This cottage never looked better."

"I love living here," she said softly, meaning it. "I'm grateful for all you've done to make it so comfortable."

Wolfe stretched a long arm to Watson, still crouched on the back of the sofa, and stroked the cat from his head to his stumpy tail. "He's still as curious as ever, I'll bet."

"Marlene thinks I'm compelled to take him with me everywhere I go," Faith said with mild sarcasm.

"Well, you know I welcome my employees' pets and the ones my guests bring along." He scratched behind Watson's ears and was rewarded with a delighted purr. "My assistant sometimes speaks before she thinks, but I do appreciate her efficiency."

There was no doubt that Marlene was scarily efficient, but she could be frustratingly contrary too. Faith kept the thought to herself and extended a hand to the plush chair she had so recently occupied. It was probably still warm from her sleepy sojourn in its comfy depths. Now Wolfe would be enclosed in it, and that thought sent a small thrill through her. "I'll be right back with the dessert and coffee. Dark roast or hazelnut?"

"Surprise me," Wolfe said with a grin.

Faith grinned too as she went to the kitchen to make coffee and arrange the brownies on two small plates. She combed her hair with her fingers and smoothed the wrinkles in her blouse before returning to the living room with a tray. She gave Wolfe a plate and a napkin and poured their coffee into her favorite lighthouse mugs, then sat across from him on the sofa. "London's not much fun traffic-wise these days, I hear," she said, imagining him commuting from his flat in Kent.

"You're right about that. It makes me appreciate Lighthouse Bay all the more. Welcoming committee aside, it is great to get home." He took a long, appreciative draft of his dark roast and fell silent.

It wasn't a troubling silence. In fact, it was refreshing to sit quietly and not have to talk. The sun slipped behind a fast-moving cloud, casting soft shadows into the cottage before reemerging to gild the top of Wolfe's head.

"I understand you and Emilie's brother were friends in college," Faith eventually said. "He told me that you went on a safari together."

Wolfe set his mug down on the end table and pressed his lips together. Several seconds elapsed before he responded. "I see Bentley found you." He closed his eyes slowly and opened them again.

"Yes, he came to the library earlier this afternoon."

He said nothing immediately, and she wondered if he had seen them leave the library, seen Bentley walk her home. And the thought sprang uninvited to her mind: *Now wouldn't it be nice if he was just the tiniest bit jealous?* Faith quickly reminded herself that she and Wolfe had no claim on each other and they were from different worlds altogether.

"That was a long time ago," Wolfe said at length, looking uncomfortable. "As for the safari, I was a green freshman and didn't know the first thing about what I was getting into. I realized shooting animals—in the wild or anywhere else—wasn't for me." He traced a slow circle around the rim of his mug. "Emilie didn't have it easy. One can understand why she built a sort of fantasy world for herself."

Faith wanted to pursue that statement, but a trinity of high-pitched beeps broke the moment.

Wolfe lifted his cell phone from his pocket and checked it. "I better take this," he said. "Sorry."

An audibly upset Marlene began talking before Wolfe had time to say hello.

"Slow down." Wolfe held the phone a few inches away from his ear. "I can't understand you. Settle down, please."

The rant didn't ease, and from her place on the sofa Faith could hear Marlene's frantic voice. "I know you had to give them access, but they've turned everything in that suite upside down! It will take our staff hours to set it right!"

"Who? What are you talking about?" Wolfe pressed the phone to his ear and leaned forward in the chair as he listened.

Faith tinkered with her mug, picked up her napkin, and swished brownie crumbs around her plate to keep herself occupied. Caring for a huge estate was a challenging task, even for the indomitable Marlene, and she wondered what had made the assistant manager so agitated. Had one of the suites been ransacked? Or did a guest leave things in a mess? Faith could no longer hear Marlene, but when she glanced at Wolfe, she noticed that his forehead was creased in anxiety.

"All right. Thank you. I'll have a word with them." Wolfe ended the call and sat holding the phone for a long moment before turning to Faith. "I'm sorry," he said, tucking the phone back into his pocket. Then he fell silent again.

"Is something wrong at the manor?" Faith asked.

"Apparently, someone left the Emily Dickinson Suite in something of a shambles. Marlene thought I might have let the police in to search the room, but I didn't." Wolfe ran a hand through his thick hair. "And they wouldn't have gone in without permission and a warrant." He stood and buttoned his suit jacket. "I thought it best not to say anything to Marlene about it, but someone might have gone into that room looking for something."

Faith felt the hairs on the back of her neck tingle. Who had been searching Emilie's room? And why? Did someone believe the validity of the documents Emilie had been bragging about for years? Someone who thought she might actually be related to Emily Dickinson? She searched Wolfe's eyes. "Do you think they were after the documents?"

He raised an eyebrow. "You said she gave them to you, right?"

Her gaze involuntarily went to the fireplace where she'd stowed the antique bag. "Yes. I told her I didn't want them, but Emilie was so insistent. She even said she'd signed a paper verifying the transfer of the documents to me. I haven't looked at them yet, but I'm taking them to the Candle House Library tomorrow to study them with my aunt."

"I'd like to keep this between you and me for now," Wolfe said in a low voice. "But just in case someone was after Emilie's documents . . ." He paused, concern etched in his eyes. "I don't want you caught in the middle of this, Faith. Please be careful."

There was something so tender in the way he looked at her that she felt her heart beat in double time. She managed to stammer, "Of course."

He nodded and gave Watson an affectionate pat on his way to the door. "Thanks for the coffee and dessert." Before stepping through the threshold, he touched her shoulder lightly, and the warmth of his fingers burned through the silk of her blouse. "It's good to be back, good to see you."

8

"I'm glad you could get away this morning," Faith told Brooke when she met her at the kitchen entrance of the mansion. "Midge will meet us at Candle House as soon as her relief staff arrives."

Brooke tucked errant strands of hair behind her ears and hooked an arm through Faith's. "Everything's covered for today's menus, but let's get going before Marlene notices I'm gone. She's on the warpath this morning."

"Anything particular sparking her fire or just the usual?" Faith asked with a grin as they walked to her SUV.

"Well, she's having a fit over the trashed Dickinson suite. Can you believe anyone would leave it in such a mess?" Brooke climbed into Faith's Honda and snapped her seat belt across her narrow hips. "Sorry to displace you, Watson," she said, smiling at the cat, who leaped over the center console and crouched obligingly in the back seat.

Faith said nothing as she revved the engine. Marlene blamed the police, but Wolfe hadn't authorized the search. Nor was it likely that Emilie had damaged the suite. It had been in immaculate order when Faith had seen it. Someone must have searched it after Emilie's departure. *I'd like to keep this between you and me for now,* Wolfe had said and urged her to be careful.

"Everyone says Emilie was eccentric and maybe a little nuts," Brooke went on, "but I can't see her destroying her room like that. She hardly had time to, did she? And the police are usually careful. Do you suppose someone else went in after Emilie died and was looking for something? Maybe the documents she talked about." She gestured to Faith's tapestry bag on the back seat.

73

Earlier that morning Faith had removed the documents Emilie had carefully stored in an acid-free plastic pouch and put them inside her own tattered tapestry tote. She had left the empty antique reticule in her cottage. "That's possible. Someone might believe the documents are genuine and try to steal them."

"I hope we'll know soon if they're real," Brooke said. "Oh, and if the destroyed suite wasn't bad enough, Marlene is afraid the guests won't want to stay. She says Emilie's death has made everyone nervous. There's been one cancellation already."

"Who was that? The cancellation?"

"Devon," she said meaningfully. "He demanded his money back too, but I don't think he got it."

Faith pictured Devon Hamlin, the odd-looking man they had met on the shore road only moments before discovering Emilie's body. Faith knew he'd been questioned by the police. He insisted he hadn't even seen the body or heard anything, human or animal. There was no evidence against him, no reason to detain him. Besides, he lived and worked in Lighthouse Bay and could be easily reached if Emilie's death was ruled anything but suicide. Still, it was unnerving to know he'd left Castleton Manor.

"But why was Devon staying at the manor when he lives in town?" Faith asked.

"Apparently, he wanted the full retreat experience." Brooke shrugged. "By the way, have you talked to Wolfe since he came back?"

Faith gave Brooke a sardonic smile. "As a matter of fact, he dropped by yesterday to say he was sorry about what happened to Emilie and that we were the ones to find her."

"That was thoughtful," she said with a sly wink. "He didn't get around to expressing his condolences to me, though."

"Don't start," Faith warned. "He was concerned because of all that trouble when I started working here. He was simply being the dutiful employer he is to everyone."

"That *was* awful for you. Diva and Bling wouldn't eat for two whole days. They just kept swimming back and forth in a daze. But the truth came out—thanks to you and your wonder cat!" Brooke glanced over her shoulder to give Watson an affectionate wink.

Faith swallowed a smile as she pulled up to the library and saw Midge heading inside with Atticus in his custom-designed basket. The Chihuahua wore expensive Doggles, glasses for his failing eyesight.

Watson scurried along beside Faith, weaving in and out of her legs, apparently unaware that he was subjecting her to possible injury. She felt a surge of joy knowing she would spend the morning with these good friends and Aunt Eileen. They would be able to help her sort through everything.

She hoped.

"What is this?" Eileen asked incredulously. She looked down at the bundle of papers withdrawn from their plastic enclosure, her forehead furrowed. "They've been folded in half! Anyone knows you don't treat archival material like that."

Faith unfolded the stack of papers with cotton-gloved fingers. Eileen had supplied gloves for each of them, knowing that finger oils could damage or destroy materials. Midge and Brooke watched as Faith carefully separated the first page from the others.

"It looks so old," Brooke remarked. "What a shame to crease it like that."

It was definitely old, the paper yellowed and slightly brittle, and Faith instantly recognized the spare, hastily scrawled part print, part script that looked like Emily Dickinson's penmanship, which was displayed prominently on the monitor Eileen had set up in advance of their morning meeting.

Midge leaned in closer, a lock of her honey-hued hair brushing Faith's cheek. "What does it say?"

"It looks like a letter. It's addressed 'Dear Friend.'" Faith scanned the broken, faded print, which remarkably had remained readable.

Dear Friend, — Vinnie asked me if I had any message for you, and while I was picking it, you ran away.

Not seeing, still we know,
Not knowing, guess;
Not guessing, smile and hide
And half caress,

And quake—and turn away;
Seraphic fear—
Is Eden's innuendo
"If you dare"?

Faith felt a kind of hush. She looked up at the other three women gathered around the table and saw an expression of amazement on their faces.

"I wonder who the friend was," Midge whispered.

"I'm not sure, but the Vinnie mentioned is Emily's sister, Lavinia," Eileen stated. "She was born three years after Emily, and they were very close. Emily also had a brother named Austin who was one year older. The three of them shared a special bond, but neither Vinnie nor Austin was quite Emily's equal in terms of intellect and creativity." She scrolled through the digital Emily Dickinson collection in the Amherst College archive on the computer. "These lines sound familiar. I think I've read them before."

"Do you suppose the friend she was writing to was Edward Smythe?" Brooke clasped her hands over her heart, her inclination for sentimentality clicking into place. She always saw the romantic side of everything. "Maybe Vinnie was their go-between."

Faith had to admit the lines were intimate, somewhat coquettish, but she was focused on the writing itself and comparing it with what she found in the archival copies. She thought it seemed remarkably close in voice and style to the Dickinson poems in the archives, yet she couldn't be sure.

"Here it is," Eileen announced, pointing to the screen where they could easily read the handwritten item with the printed version directly across the digital page.

"'Dear Friend,'" Midge began excitedly, "'Vinnie asked me if I had any message . . .' Why, it's the same letter!"

"Yes," Eileen said firmly, sweeping back her shoulder-length brown hair. "It's Amherst Manuscript #56, and it was written to a Mrs. Edward Tuckerman. See? There's the inscription. We can cross-check it with the Boston collection, but I'm sure we'll find it the same. Emilie would have had ample opportunity to access the collection. And of course, anyone can view these documents online."

"Even though it looks old, it could have been made to look old," Brooke said glumly. Absently, she tugged on one of her earrings. "I was reading on the Internet the other day seven ways to antique your paper. Brushing coffee or tea on crumpled paper and then baking it in the oven can do wonders if you want to fool someone."

"I suppose the letter could have been made to look old," Faith said thoughtfully. "Emilie Smythe may have copied this herself, maybe convinced herself that it was written to her great-great-grandfather. She wanted so much to believe it. The little curls on the lowercase *n* look a little different from Dickinson's."

"You could be right, Faith," Eileen said. "We'll need a real expert to test the paper this is written on, to authenticate that it was really written in the 1800s."

They waded through the sheets and half sheets of paper, comparing them with extant documents. In almost every case, they found them to be copies of poems and letters already in the archives.

Faith felt a pervading sadness. Had Emilie Smythe's life been so joyless, so without comfort, that she needed to immerse herself in another's?

Brooke gently handed Faith a page she had been reading. "These lines are lovely and might have been written to someone the poet cared a great deal for." She cleared her throat, but the lines still came out husky with feeling.

> *I taught my Heart a hundred times*
> *Precisely what to say—*
> *Provoking Lover, when you came*
> *Its Treatise flew away*
> *To hide my strategy too late*
> *To wiser be too soon—*
> *For miseries so halcyon*
> *The happiness atone—*

Faith nodded. "Those are some of Dickinson's loveliest lines, and I memorized them long ago. But who can say precisely what she meant by them?" She faced Eileen. "It was unlikely that we'd find anything to prove Emilie's claims, but at least we have given them careful consideration."

"What now?" Midge asked, clasping her hands together. She had removed the cotton gloves, and her fingernails boasted little cat faces with pink noses painted on them. "How about coffee and some of those homemade peanut butter cookies I spied on your desk, Eileen?"

"By all means, let's have coffee and cookies," Eileen answered, then turned to Faith, who was still pondering the documents. "Why don't you leave these with me? I'll put them in the safe here, and as time permits I'll go over them again just to make sure we haven't missed anything. Is that all right with you?"

Faith felt a great sense of relief. For some reason she couldn't name, the pitiful bits of poetry and fragmented prose saddened her. She hadn't looked forward to taking the collection back to the cottage. "That's a good idea. Thanks, Aunt Eileen." She started stacking the pages and for the first time noticed a half sheet of paper much whiter than the others. "This is odd," she remarked as she scanned the page. "It doesn't sound like Dickinson or even Emilie Smythe. And as for being from the nineteenth century, no way. It's typewritten. Cambria 12 point."

"Probably something Emilie stuck in there by mistake," Brooke offered. "Maybe she got mixed up."

Faith silently read the short lines.

The lighthouse at ten.
Prithee don't fail me.
The saints are watching—
anon they hail thee.

She passed the paper to the others. "What do you make of that?"

"It's Victorian language—that's for sure," Midge said. "*Prithee* and *anon*?" The lighthouse here at Lighthouse Bay? Who were the saints, and what were they watching for?"

"I'll keep this one," Faith said, intrigued, and tucked it into her jacket that was draped over the back of her chair. "Ouch!" She yanked her hand out of the pocket, then carefully removed the fishing lure she had taken from Watson's fur the day Emilie had died. It was green and rubbery, painted with blue fins and a stark black eye. The sharp hook had poked her finger, and she wiped a drop of blood away.

"What's that?" Midge asked, grinning. "I didn't know you like to fish. Have you been playing hooky and didn't invite us?"

Faith stared at the garish thing in her palm. A bit of lint from her pocket was caught in the hook. "I haven't worn this anorak since that day when we were walking along the shore road." She looked up at her friends. "I saw it in Watson's hindquarters and pulled it off before it could hurt him. In the trauma of what had happened to Emilie, I just stuck it in my pocket and never gave it another thought." Faith shivered, remembering the way the waves had swirled and eddied around the body.

Eileen took it gingerly and turned it over. "Very distinctive," she murmured, "but no one fishes in that area. Still, it could have washed up along the rocks, I suppose. Maybe you should mention it to Chief Garris."

Faith wrapped the lure in her scarf and put it back in her jacket pocket. "Did someone say peanut butter cookies?"

Atticus made a short yipping sound and sat up in the basket by Midge's feet. The Chihuahua's ears stood up comically, dislodging his very expensive dog glasses.

At the same time, Watson appeared from the adjacent room where he liked to sit in a sunny window and came padding toward Faith, greedy eyes alert.

"Who says animals don't understand our language?" Midge declared, picking up Atticus and replacing his Doggles. She kissed him on his little brown nose. "But your treats are in my purse. No peanut butter cookies for you."

"Or you, Mr. Watson, sir," Faith chided good-naturedly. "I have it on good authority that Eileen keeps a supply of tunaroons in her desk. Behave yourself and she just might dig one out for you." She leaned down to stroke his arched back. "But we've taken up too much of Eileen's time. Besides, tonight is the poetry reading in the library. Brooke and I have to get back."

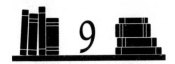

9

Faith looked forward to the evening's poetry reading, which Marlene had asked her to host in the Castleton library. Members were scheduled to read their original poems, which would be followed by music from a string quartet and special refreshments. That was Brooke's department. The poetry reading wasn't exactly a black-tie event, but most of the guests would likely dress up, so Faith wore a black calf-length dress.

The library had been prepared for an evening of relaxation, poetry, and music. A cheery fire burned low and steady in the great main fireplace. Candles flamed in silver wall sconces and on low tables, and the comfortable crimson sofas and chairs were arranged for cozy camaraderie. The retreat guests gathered in subdued groups, perhaps rehearsing in their minds the poems they would share. Of course, the death of one of their members could not help but impact the atmosphere for these sensitive poetry lovers.

What would Emilie have shared? Because of her affinity for Dickinson, her lines probably would have emulated the famous poet's style. Or they may have been unique, perhaps surprising them all. Undoubtedly, she would have dressed in white.

Faith glanced around the room and spotted Bentley on the second floor of the library. He stood next to a shorter, slender man with a dark mustache and a crop of curly black hair tightly restrained and tied back. He had smooth olive skin not unlike Bentley's. A relative? An acquaintance? Or maybe a guest of the retreat Faith hadn't seen before? The stranger wore a black nylon jacket and jeans. Obviously, he had no intention of participating in the dressy event. Suddenly he disappeared with a nod and a quick turning of his lithe body, leaving Bentley alone.

After a few moments, Bentley's eyes connected with hers. Connected and lingered.

Faith looked away from his intimate gaze and realized Marlene was at the podium. As usual, the assistant manager was impeccably dressed in a long-skirted suit of pale green that matched the color of her eyes. Her fair hair was drawn back in her signature chignon, banded with something that glittered in the light when she moved.

"Welcome, everyone," Marlene said, keeping some distance between herself and the microphone, as though worried that if she got too close it might reach out and grab her. She was clearly not at ease speaking in front of a group, but it was her duty to get the evening started. "Our resident librarian, Miss Newberry, will host this evening's festivities," Marlene announced in her short, clipped accents. "I'm sure we will all be enriched by her scholarship and creative endeavors." With that, she nodded stiffly toward Faith and swept away from the podium.

Faith took her place at the microphone. "Why do we love poetry?" she asked, gazing into the faces around her. "Perhaps because poetry is natural. It's fundamental. You and I were poets in our cribs when we babbled sounds for the sheer joy of hearing them. Hunters and gatherers around the campfire told their tales in poetry, the most primal fashion they knew. In every age, where there are people, there is speech. And where there is speech, there is poetry."

The door opened with a soft *click*, admitting a latecomer into the library. Wolfe, wearing a dark suit, entered quietly and took a seat in the back row of chairs.

Faith felt a quickening in her stomach. Wolfe didn't always attend these evening events, even when he was in residence at Castleton. When their glances touched, she took a steadying breath and continued. "Of course, there are those who find poetry esoteric and perhaps superfluous. The education landscape often deemphasizes creative expression in favor of expository writing. Yet poetry teaches students how to write, read, and understand more fully. It also provides a healthy outlet for surging emotions. But I don't need to convince you of the merits of poetry. You know, as Mandelstam did, that people need poetry as they need bread."

A diminutive lady seated close to the podium nodded approvingly. She held her hands primly in her lap on top of a small loose-leaf notebook and wore a trim navy suit that rendered the stark whiteness of her hair almost fluorescent. Her name tag read *Martha Weathers*.

Faith realized the woman was to be the first reader. *The retired teacher from New Brunswick*, she recalled and imagined the lady intoning the merits of poetry to sports-minded high school boys and romance-ridden girls.

Next to Martha sat Wilhelmina Hodge, the sullen young woman from the welcome dinner who had openly disapproved of Emilie Smythe's claims to kinship with the poet of Amherst. *Someone should put a stop to that woman's rumors.* Wilhelmina was a curious name for someone in her twenties. Faith watched Martha whisper something in Wilhelmina's ear and pat one of her trembling white hands. She noticed that Wilhelmina's fingernails had been bitten down to the quick.

Pushing away the distraction, Faith went on. "The nature of poetry follows from our own human nature. Imagery, emotional expression, sound, rhythm, and sense all work together to form a complete work that speaks to the emotions and the mind." After a few more remarks and recognition of the stringed quartet, Faith took a step back from the podium. "Now, let's welcome Martha Weathers, who will be reading her poem 'Lady November.'"

Martha rose and walked to the front in her sturdy brogues. Perhaps she would present something sentimental with archaic syntax. Faith scanned the faces of the audience and read expressions ranging from embarrassment to boredom. A few guests cleared their throats or coughed daintily. She gave Martha an encouraging smile. *Poets have to be a hearty lot*, Faith thought, *especially those willing to share their work with a critical peer group.*

The schoolteacher opened her notebook but focused on something just over the heads of the seated guests. Her voice rang mellow but strong. "The title of my poem is 'Lady November.'" She touched her handkerchief to her lips briefly and started to recite: "'Elegant and fine, she begins her slow dance.'"

A middle-aged gentleman who had been dozing off in front of the fire snapped to attention. Several other sets of eyes widened with interest. Martha continued.

She has turned all but the last lamp down
and moves with a catlike grace.
She drops her crimson cape and folds it soft away.
Her hair falls like a silken drape.
She hesitates in the gathering gloom,
hugs herself with trembling arms.
A tear escapes. She reaches for the last glowing lamp
as night falls.

A hush fell like a whispering cloud as Martha Weathers closed her notebook and returned to her seat.

Rousing applause followed, along with murmurs of "Beautiful," "Compelling," and "Hear, hear" as the audience delighted in the colorful expression of late autumn.

The next reader was Wilhelmina Hodge. She crept up to the podium like a doomed victim to the gallows, the vague menthol scent Faith had first detected at the welcome dinner following her. She announced the title of her poem without looking up. "'Daddy's Visit.'"

After a few seconds of silence, she began.

He swept into my room on the weeping winter wind.
Night frost glazed his cheeks, shimmered in his eyes.
Silent, lest he leave me, I lay quite still

'Til at last his breath came spinning
With sweet-sour wine and whispers,
With songs too sad for singing,
With promises unpromised.
He drew a furry treasure from the pocket of his coat
And tucked it warm beside me in the cradle of my arms.
He touched me with his eyes, then vanished into night.
I hugged the little kitten—hugged it 'til it cried,
And I cried with childish passion
And longed for him instead.

There was a prolonged silence as everyone absorbed the surprising pathos of the poem. For Faith, it was especially touching, as she thought about finding Watson in a difficult period in her life and how the cat had bolstered her confidence. The poem likely involved much more for Wilhelmina. A family rift that caused a child to bleed emotionally? What inner scars had been left behind to match the ones on her face? But there was no time to ruminate further on the strange young woman and her antipathy to Emilie Smythe.

Several more poems were read. A few were quite lengthy, but each found enthusiastic response.

Soon they were down to the last reader—Jerold Carter, a dignified man in his early sixties. He announced the title of his poem in a clear Boston accent: "'A Visit to the Doctor.'" Jerold didn't have anything in his hands to read, so he gazed out at the audience as he recited:

There's a wizard in my bones
Who knows the answer to the riddle.
But he's seldom given to speech
And likes to keep me in the middle.
He's unimpressed with my suggestions,
My attempts to apprehend him.

Still, I'd like to find his castle,
Appeal to some quirk or whim
That would set his dull tongue loose.
I do not ask for special favor,
Just a kind of settled truce
And less bizarre behavior.

He bowed low and strode back to his seat amidst loud clapping.

Marlene was almost beaming. Evidently, the evening was turning out much better than she anticipated when she'd issued the assignment to Faith. Her words had rankled: "I trust you'll come up with something to keep us from being bored to death."

Faith gave her boss a piquant glance. Genuine expression from hearts attuned to the magic of words was anything but dull.

The quartet launched into a piece from Vivaldi's *The Four Seasons*—appropriately, they'd chosen "Spring"—and the guests moved toward the refreshment table, where Brooke and another manor employee named Laura uncovered plates of fancy sandwiches and delectable-looking sweets.

Faith sidled up to Brooke. "This looks fantastic. You've outdone yourself."

Brooke coiled a strand of hair behind her ear. She, too, had dressed for the occasion in a simple but elegant wraparound dress that drew out the blue in her eyes. "I was listening from the anteroom. That was so enjoyable. *You've* outdone yourself," she added, parroting Faith's compliment.

"It's amazing what subjects and styles poets come up with. Some are very unlike what you'd expect," Faith said, helping herself to a triangle of dark rye spread with something creamy and topped with artichoke. "At first, everyone was rather gloomy and quiet, but they came to life once the poems started."

"Did you see that handsome guy, the one watching from the second floor?" Brooke asked conspiratorially.

Trust Brooke to zero in on an attractive man, Faith thought. "Which one?"

"The one up there," she said, pointing to the upper balcony. "Tall, elegantly dressed, dark hair, smoldering gaze."

"Emilie's brother, Bentley Smythe," Faith answered. Obviously, Brooke hadn't noticed there had been two men, though Bentley was more attractive, and the other man had not been there long. "He's staying here while arrangements are made."

Marlene strode over and circled the table, peering into each offering to make sure it accorded with her standards. She nodded to guests, treating some to a tight smile.

Brooke glanced at the assistant manager, then whispered to Faith, "Is he single?"

When Faith didn't reply, Brooke repeated, "Mr. Smythe. Is he single?"

"I think so," Faith responded. "I only met him yesterday when he stopped in at the library."

Brooke craned her neck to search the upper floor and murmured, "I was hoping he'd come down for refreshments, but he seems to have disappeared."

Along with that man in the black nylon jacket, Faith thought. She must ask Marlene who he was. Something in the man's furtive movements had troubled her.

Brooke returned her attention to Faith, a slight smile on her lips. "And guess who else is here to take in the evening hosted by the resident librarian, who I might add looks especially beautiful tonight?" She motioned toward a small group of men near the fireplace.

Faith turned to see Wolfe mingling with the guests, his head rising above all the others. Light from the fireplace caught the silver highlights at his temples. He was magnificent in his dark suit, his hands held loosely in his pockets, but she also noticed that he appeared vaguely tired or perhaps worried. He was conscientious in looking after the family's financial interests, but Faith wished he could delegate more. She mused that if only he didn't have to travel so much, Wolfe might extend his stays at Castleton. She felt her cheeks grow warm and deliberately turned back to Brooke, who was eyeing her mischievously.

"He doesn't usually come to these retreat soirees," Brooke said, winking at Faith. "I'm just sayin'."

A voice broke in. "I certainly hope you have more of these sandwiches." Marlene shook a finger in Brooke's face and scowled. "That tray is almost empty. Apparently, writing poetry gives one an enormous appetite."

"There are plenty more," Brooke said, whipping around. "Laura, bring another tray, please."

The staffer, who had been the target of Marlene's invective before, nearly stumbled over her feet in her rush to obey.

"We have everything under control," Brooke said, her voice calm. She gave Marlene a reassuring smile. Brooke had a way of facing up to her demanding boss that defused difficult situations.

Suddenly a gasp came from Marlene's lips. Her body went rigid, and her eyes sharpened like daggers. "Not the police again." Her voice shook. "Not here!"

Faith looked to the rear of the library and spotted Chief Andy Garris standing just inside the door, his uniform clearly outlined by the candlelight glowing on his bald head. That the chief had come in person during a scheduled event was not a good sign, but at least he hadn't brought a contingent with him.

Marlene seemed rooted to the spot, so Faith hurried over to Wolfe. She touched his arm and gestured to the library entrance.

Instantly, he made his way toward the chief with Faith following close at his side. "Good evening, Andy," Wolfe greeted him.

"Good to see you, Wolfe," Chief Garris said, then nodded to Faith. "Glad you're here too. I need to speak with both of you and Miss Milner. Is there somewhere we can talk?" His words were measured but low. The chief was sensitive enough not to make a scene in front of all the guests, a trait that garnered Faith's respect.

"Yes, my office," Wolfe offered, then asked Faith to fetch Brooke.

As the foursome were about to enter Wolfe's office, Faith heard quick steps behind them. She turned to see Bentley Smythe approaching them.

"You have confirmed the cause of my sister's death?" he asked the chief. The edge to his voice might have been due to anxiety or grief. Or was he offended that he hadn't been contacted first? But who had known where he was? Faith hadn't seen him since before the readings.

The chief looked puzzled, his sharp eyes measuring Bentley.

"I'm Bentley Smythe, Emilie's brother as well as her guardian," he said, introducing himself. "The family has been waiting for results of the autopsy. What is taking so long? We're anxious to put this terrible business behind us."

"I see," Chief Garris said slowly as he studied Bentley. "I understand Mr. Jaxon advised you of your sister's death. Where were you at that time, Mr. Smythe?"

"I was returning from a business trip to Hong Kong," he replied, a defensive note in his voice. "What's this all about?"

"Let's take this inside," Wolfe said, frowning. He closed the door after them and gestured for them to sit. His expansive office held a conference table as well as a more relaxed grouping of chairs near the fireplace. It was to these that Wolfe shepherded them, seating himself last.

The chief regarded each of them, obviously alert to nuances only he could have defined. At last he said quietly, "Miss Smythe's death has been ruled suspicious. Bruises were identified on her body—particularly her upper arms and shoulders. These indicate coercion or mistreatment occurred within a short time of her death. There were no discernible fingerprints, but we don't believe Miss Smythe was alone on that ledge."

Faith felt her heart stop. *Who could have done this? And why?*

Next to her, Bentley gasped and dropped his head in his hands— hands that visibly trembled.

Instinctively, she touched his arm. "Are you all right?" she whispered. The question felt foolish, but she didn't know what else to say.

He didn't answer. Presently, he lifted his head, grief written on his face. "But who? Who would want to hurt her?"

"We're going to do everything we can to find out," the chief responded. "We will learn what happened to Miss Smythe."

The white clapboard building that housed the Lighthouse Bay police force blended well with the local architecture. The only things that gave away its purpose were the cruisers parked out back and the antennas on the roof. It had been a while since Faith had entered its doors, but all the same, it was too familiar. She seemed to have a knack for getting involved in police matters. At least this time she wasn't considered a suspect.

Chief Garris's visit the evening before had changed everything. Faith hadn't thought anything could be worse than a woman accidentally or purposefully falling off a rocky ledge and drowning at Castleton Manor. But knowing that someone might have been responsible for Emilie's death was infinitely worse. Everyone had gone home with heavy hearts and with the awareness that someone at the retreat—invited or not—posed a significant danger.

Faith had locked her cottage doors and welcomed the warm presence of Watson, who seemed especially attentive to her mood. He hadn't budged from her bed all night. In the morning, she gave him an extra ration of his favorite breakfast food and promised they'd both pay a visit to Carlo, the Newfoundland who'd become Watson's cohort. She hoped the kennel staff was treating the forlorn creature well.

Daphne Kerrigan, the attractive and efficient receptionist, peered over her tortoiseshell glasses and waved hello. "He's ready for you, Faith," she called, placing her hand over the receiver of the phone. "Nice to see you again."

As nice as it was to see the amiable Daphne, she wished their meetings didn't involve crime and mayhem. Faith walked to the chief's open door and knocked.

"Thanks for coming by so promptly," the chief said, rising to greet her. The former marine towered over his desk, and even in his shirtsleeves he evoked a formidable respect. But his blue eyes were kind as he extended a rough, warm hand.

Something about Andy Garris always made Faith think of her father. A retired Springfield, Massachusetts, police sergeant, Martin Newberry was tall and outgoing and possessed a generous heart. And he was free with his hugs where his family was concerned. What she wouldn't do to feel his big arms around her right now.

"Have a seat," Garris said, snapping her out of her reverie. He indicated the chair across from his desk, then sat down. "How are you holding up?"

"These last few days have been pretty rough. So much has happened and all of it confusing." Faith sighed and dropped into the chair. "I'm so sorry to hear that someone wanted to hurt Emilie Smythe. *Did* hurt her," she amended, shaking her head.

The chief pushed a button on a tape recorder in the center of his desk and leaned back in his chair.

Upon his request and for the record, she retold the events of the morning she and Brooke and Midge had found Emilie, of the body lying half in and half out of the water with Carlo guarding her. The image seemed even worse knowing someone was responsible for her death. The bruises had been typical of someone pressing their fingers into her upper arms, Garris had said. Or had someone been trying to restrain her, keep her from going over? But where had Carlo been? Why hadn't he protected her?

"And you saw no one except Mr. Hamlin near the scene?" the chief asked.

"That's right. We met him along the shore road."

The police had questioned Hamlin already, but he would likely remain a person of interest. It didn't help his case that he'd left Castleton Manor before the retreat ended. Hamlin insisted he didn't know Emilie and had not seen the body, but was he telling the truth? She shivered thinking about it. Did the antique dealer have a reason to murder Emilie? Had he returned to the scene of the crime, having killed her a few hours earlier? And if he had, would Carlo have stayed silent?

The chief's voice interrupted her bleak thoughts. "We need to know more about the documents Miss Smythe gave you. They could have a bearing on this case, especially in view of the ransacked suite. Ms. Russell blamed us, thinking we had searched it, but it wasn't our doing. And unless Miss Smythe left the room in shambles, someone was obviously looking for something. Someone who wore gloves and didn't leave any fingerprints."

Faith described being summoned to Emilie's suite during the welcome dinner and how Emilie had insisted that she take the documents. "She has claimed for years that her great-great-grandmother was Emily Dickinson. Yet there's nothing in the historical records or scholarship to give that idea any credence at all."

"Yes, most people around here are aware of Miss Smythe's eccentricities." He peered at her, his sharp blue eyes intense. "Why do you think she gave the documents to you?"

Faith shook her head. "She's known to be difficult and overbearing, hard to get along with, but that night she seemed different. I think she was afraid of something. Or someone. Or maybe she was just tired of the pretense of being related to the famous poet by blood. She wouldn't take no for an answer and absolutely insisted that I take the documents."

"Where are the papers now?" the chief asked. "If that's what someone wanted, they may well go looking for them again."

"They're in the safe at the Candle House Library. I showed them to Aunt Eileen because she's very knowledgeable about these things." Faith told him about studying the documents with her friends and not coming to a clear conclusion. "You can have them, Chief," she said, even though she knew he had only to demand they be turned over. "No warrant required. They're all there, except this one." She withdrew the note from her purse and handed it to him. "This one was different."

The lighthouse at ten.
Prithee don't fail me.
The saints are watching—
anon they hail thee.

As Chief Garris read the note he pushed out his jaw in obvious consternation. "What on earth? Nobody talks like that now."

"But it's typewritten on modern paper. It also sounds a little like some sort of threat."

He nodded. "Any idea what it could mean?"

"None whatsoever."

"Well, I'm glad you brought it in." He stood in one fluid motion, then slipped the note into a manila folder and clicked off the recorder. "We'll hang on to those documents. No need to put Candle House or your aunt in danger. And, of course, if you uncover any pertinent information, I'll expect you to share it." He gave her a stern look. "But that doesn't mean you have carte blanche to go investigating on your own. I don't want you to get hurt."

Faith left the police station feeling only slightly more at ease than when she'd entered. She had told Chief Garris everything she could, including information about the documents Emilie had given her. She was glad they were safe at Candle House and no longer in her possession, and soon they'd be in the hands of the police. Whoever had been looking for them in the Emily Dickinson Suite was cautious enough to wear gloves and not leave a trace. That wasn't the kind of thief she wanted to tangle with.

She had every confidence in Chief Garris and in his officers, but there wasn't much to go on. No footprints or clues that hadn't been washed away by the unremitting waves splashing on the rock. And what could the bruises on Emilie's body tell about the person who had been with her on that ledge? Had he or she killed Emilie or tried to keep her from ending her life?

She decided to stop at Happy Tails Bakery to purchase treats for Watson and Carlo. She parked and hurried to the door. What she really wanted was to see Midge's friendly face. She needed the strength of her friends.

When Faith opened the door of the bakery, she was met by an excited Atticus, his Doggles bobbing on his little head. She knelt to pet the nearsighted Chihuahua just as Midge came out from the back.

"Oh, it's you!" Midge exclaimed. "He got past me when I wasn't looking. Good thing you aren't a customer." She gathered Atticus up in her arms. She was generally careful to keep the rambunctious dog out of the way of customers.

"But I am." Faith laughed, pleased to see both Midge and Atticus. "I need some tunaroons for Watson and whatever you suggest for Carlo. Maybe the strawberry pup-tarts."

"I can take care of that. But sit down first. I'll return Atticus to his digs, and we'll have some coffee." Midge cradled the dog and gave him a kiss on the top of his tiny head. "Sarah's finishing up in the back. She'll handle customers while we talk."

In record time, she returned bearing a tray of fresh scones. "Grab some coffee from the sideboard, will you? There's hazelnut brewing."

Faith brought two cups and sat down opposite Midge. "You've got flour in your hair," she said, grinning.

Midge chuckled as she ran a hand through her hair. "So how are you doing?"

Faith quickly sobered. "I've been at loose ends ever since we found out Emilie's death has been ruled suspicious." While Midge hadn't been at Castleton last night when the news of possible foul play broke, Faith had phoned her right away. "And I've just come from the police station."

"You poor thing," Midge said kindly. "I gave my statement earlier. I can think of dozens of things more fun than that."

"Yes, like getting a root canal or a dressing-down from Marlene."

"Did the chief say whether they have a line on a suspect?" Midge asked.

"No, but you know how the chief is. He's not going to comment on the case, but he asked if we'd seen anyone besides Devon Hamlin near the scene. Leaving Castleton before the retreat is over makes him look guilty. I think the guy has a good deal of explaining to do." She nibbled on her scone without tasting it. "Do you suppose Devon could have done something like that? He says he didn't even know Emilie."

Midge tapped her long nails on the table. She was wearing what she called "horse tails" today—amber curlicues that swirled along half of each nail. "I think he's kind of creepy."

"He can't help that his ears stick out and that he has red hair," Faith protested. "He's probably just what he seems, a business owner who likes poetry and who just happened to be near the place where Emilie died."

"Devon does some jewelry repair on the side. It's one way to get patrons into his shop, entice them to view his antiques." Midge sat up straighter in her chair and narrowed her eyes. "You know, I just happen to have a bracelet with a broken clasp. I should probably have it repaired." She raised an eyebrow at Faith.

"Are you suggesting we drop in and see him on his own turf?"

"Exactly. Devon's shop is just a hop, skip, and jump down the road, honey," she drawled. "How about we go calling?"

"Right now?"

Midge smiled. "My daddy always said, 'Now's the best time to do what needs doing.'"

"I still have a little more time before I have to get back to the manor," Faith said, already feeling the adrenaline pumping.

Midge had been right. They jumped into Faith's Honda and in less than five minutes pulled up alongside Hamlin's Antiques. The tasteful building blended in with the others just off the main street.

Faith glanced through the front window and didn't see anyone inside. "Looks quiet."

"All the better," Midge said, slinging her purse over her shoulder and heading to the door with a purposeful step.

The store boasted no customers, nor could they see any employees. Faith and Midge perused gleaming display cases with feigned interest and presently heard someone emerge from a back room. When Faith turned around, she caught her breath.

The lanky man with protruding ears and close-cropped red hair greeted them wearing an enormous pair of dark glasses. "Good morning, ladies. May I help—?" Devon broke off in the middle of the sentence and seemed to grow rigid behind the counter.

"Hello, Mr. Hamlin. It's nice to see you again. I'm Faith Newberry, the librarian at Castleton Manor. We met—" She stopped herself. She hardly needed to remind him that they'd met along the shore road the morning Emilie had been found dead.

He frowned and grunted something unintelligible. It was disconcerting not to see the man's eyes. Why was he wearing dark glasses inside?

"I have a bracelet that needs a new clasp," Midge told him, digging into her large bag. "I hear you do excellent work. I was wondering if you could repair it for me."

Devon reached for it with his left hand and winced. He jerked his hand back and held it stiffly against his side, then used his right hand to take the bracelet.

He's been hurt, Faith realized. She'd be willing to bet those glasses perched on his beak of a nose concealed a black eye. She looked away to hide her startled reaction, grateful for Midge's animated commentary on how much she loved the bracelet and how she missed wearing it.

Glancing around the shop, Faith noticed that one of the glass cases was covered with a sheet or a tarp of some kind and that the entrance to the antiques showroom had been closed off with a heavy curtain. She leaned in toward Devon. "Are you all right?"

He put the bracelet down on the counter and stared at her, the pallor of his complexion exaggerated by the dark glasses. "I'm fine," he answered too quickly.

Faith and Midge continued to watch him.

Then Devon let out an exasperated sigh. "All right," he snapped, ripping off the glasses, "I fell down some stairs. But it's no big deal." Devon's left eye and the bridge of his nose were deeply bruised.

Faith sucked in her breath. It looked terribly painful and accentuated his bizarre features. "Oh! I'm sorry. This has been quite a week for you. First Emilie Smythe's death and then—"

"Yes, and I've had my fill of questions from the police. I trust I won't have to endure any more from you." His response bordered on rudeness, but Faith couldn't blame him. After all, he had been interrogated on at least two occasions that she knew of.

"We've been questioned too. It seems to me that those of us who just happened to be in the area where Emilie was found should stick together." Faith raised her eyebrows meaningfully. "After all, none of us had a reason to want to hurt her." She wanted to add, *did we*? But he would hardly own up to it if he was guilty.

Frowning, Devon fumbled under the counter with his right hand, pulled out a pad of paper, and scribbled on it. He handed the receipt to Midge. "Just leave the bracelet with me. It should be ready for you early next week."

Midge smiled like the gracious belle she was. "Well, thank you, Mr. Hamlin. I'll see you then."

His mouth, capacious in his narrow face, remained fixed in a frown.

"I hope you feel better soon," Faith said, heading for the door. How she wished she could peek behind that curtain. Had whatever happened to Devon involved an attack here in his own shop?

She shivered as they stepped out into the cool air. If he had been attacked, she could bet he probably hadn't reported it to the police. Did it have anything to do with Emilie Smythe?

11

Faith drove home after dropping Midge off at Happy Tails Bakery. Midge was preparing to leave that afternoon for a short convention, and Faith was looking forward to a quiet lunch at her cottage with Watson for company. He would ask no questions and would be glad to see her. Even if he pretended indifference, his snit wouldn't last very long. He would soon wind himself around her legs and entreat her to feed him. Then, after library hours, they would visit Carlo.

What she hadn't expected was to find a fuming Marlene on her doorstep, arms crossed over her belted trench coat. "Where have you been? I've been trying to reach you all morning!" The assistant manager's nostrils flared indignantly as she tapped her left foot on the stone step.

Taken aback, Faith gawked at her, unsure how to respond. She wasn't scheduled to be in the library until one, and it was barely noon. Did Marlene expect her to outline her personal schedule for the day? Besides, her cell hadn't rung all morning. She pulled it from her pocket, remembering that there had been only one bar remaining when she'd last checked. Oh no. It was dead. "I'm sorry. I meant to charge it when I left the police station."

"That's very unprofessional of you," Marlene admonished. "We expect our staff to be available when they're needed. You should have learned that by now."

Had Marlene gotten up on the wrong side of the bed this morning? Something seemed to be sticking in Marlene's craw, but Faith had to admit being unreachable was careless of her. She took a key from her purse and proceeded to unlock the door. She turned back to Marlene. "Do you want to come in?"

A loud meow came through the front window. Watson was perched on the back of the couch looking out at them—or was it glowering? *Definitely glowering.* Faith sighed. She didn't feel particularly popular at the moment.

"Thank you, but I don't think so," Marlene said, returning Watson's glare. "I'm not ready to be pounced on by that animal of yours."

"Watson won't pounce on you. He's a gentleman." Faith couldn't help baiting her. When was Marlene going to get around to stating her reason for being on her doorstep?

"When I couldn't reach you, I decided to come over and leave you a note. You'll recall that Martha Weathers is on the schedule to give an informal lecture in the dining room tonight. Something about the place of poetry in education. She agreed to take the slot we'd reserved for Emilie Smythe's lecture on Dickinson."

Faith remembered Martha Weathers, the woman whose poem about autumn had kicked off the reading. "That's a relief," Faith said, wondering what any of this had to do with her.

"She needs to gather additional information for her lecture and is anxious for some assistance in the library. She asked specifically for you."

"It couldn't wait until one o'clock?" Faith was incredulous.

"We try to accommodate our guests here," Marlene said with a good deal of sarcasm. "I thought it wouldn't hurt you to come in a bit early so she could gather the material she needs. Without said material we might end up with a mediocre program, and that would be very bad for business." She pressed a hand to her hair. The wind had torn a few blonde tendrils from her chignon. "And we don't do mediocre."

Surely someone else could have steered the woman to the educational stats or whatever she needed. But Martha had asked for her, and Faith had to admit that piqued her interest. "Give me fifteen minutes and I'll be there."

"Good," Marlene said with a graceless harrumph. She scowled at Watson before stalking away.

Why Marlene worked at Castleton where the pets she seemed to despise accompanied their guests was a mystery to Faith. Sometimes she thought there was something of a love-hate relationship between Watson and the assistant manager. They'd had their run-ins, like the time Watson had landed in the middle of her desk, sending papers and Marlene herself flying, which had admittedly been a pounce. Faith had told Marlene then that Watson actually liked her and that was why he tried to get under her skin.

The cat watched the human storm off. Maybe her clothes were too tight or she'd eaten something sour this morning. Undoubtedly, she thought she owned the place and his human as well.

But she couldn't push him around. He had his ways, and he was a lot quicker than she was. He raised his head to make himself as tall as possible. Maybe he could sneak out. One quick pounce? It had been such fun before . . . He felt the claws on his right paw twitching. Wouldn't it be amusing to snatch that round yellow ball at the back of her head and bat it around for a while? He could grab it in a flash. She'd never catch him.

When his human came inside he sat stone-still on the back of the couch, his nose in the air to prove he wasn't in a hurry. Did she say tunaroons? Ah, well! With a tempered meow, he scampered down from the couch.

Faith grabbed a sandwich and gave Watson his tunaroons, and then the two of them set off for the library. Watson was not about to be locked in the cottage for the afternoon. She hoped Martha Weathers had a greater affinity for cats than Marlene did. "You will be good, won't you, Watson?" she asked him affectionately.

The cat merely looked at her, green eyes innocent.

The library, with its lovely ambience and inviting shelves, was quiet. It was still the lunch hour, so no guests were likely to appear other than Martha, whose impending visit Marlene had arbitrarily arranged. Faith drank in the silence, feeling instantly at home and satisfied in an inexplicable way.

Watson sauntered off to inspect the area as he always did, ears erect, whiskers twitching with anticipation.

She'd been settled at her desk for only a few moments when the door to the library opened.

Martha was dressed more casually than at the poetry reading in a gray wool skirt, a white blouse, and a pale blue cardigan. Her leather brogues completed the schoolmarm outfit, but her unlined face and confident step made her appear younger than she probably was. Soft white curls framed her face in a style that, though reminiscent of earlier years, was nonetheless attractive. She approached Faith and sat down abruptly in the chair opposite the desk.

Faith stood and extended her hand. "Hello, Mrs. Weathers. I wanted to tell you how much I enjoyed your poem at the reading last night. The lines were as lovely as they were surprising. I hope you're finding worthy outlets for your fine work."

"Thank you," she said, her brown eyes shining. "I have had some of my poems published, but my main work has been closely tied to teaching and the classroom. I want to present poetry so young people will be enriched by it and embrace it for life."

Faith felt instant admiration for the elderly teacher from New Brunswick and recalled how she had patted Wilhelmina's hand and whispered what must have been encouragement in her ear. "I wanted to thank you as well for helping to steady the nerves of the young lady who was sitting next to you. Wilhelmina, wasn't it? Everyone enjoyed her poem about her daddy's visit."

"She likes to be called Willa," Martha clarified. "She's a great aficionado of the poet of Amherst. Emilie Smythe's claims upset her, and she disapproves of Emilie's insinuation that Dickinson was involved with a married man." She shook her head. "Willa's had a hard life. A sad, hard life." She fell silent, apparently not about to elaborate on the sad, hard life of Miss Hodge.

Several questions sprang to Faith's mind. How well did Wilhelmina and Emilie know each other? Had she known Emilie would be at the retreat and that she would be giving a lecture on Dickinson? Were the police aware of their connection and of Wilhelmina's antipathy? Faith considered the bits of conversation she had overheard the night she waited at the Dickinson table. Was it possible that shy young woman could have been involved in Emilie's death? It seemed ludicrous that the fragile Wilhelmina might be strong enough to leave bruises on a body.

"Well," she said, smiling warmly at Martha, "I can see that you are a great encourager."

The compliment seemed to embarrass Martha. She stared down at her hands and didn't say anything for a long moment.

"I understand you need to review some materials in preparation for your presentation tonight," Faith said, changing the subject to ease the tension. "How can I help you?"

Martha looked directly at Faith. "I'm afraid I have prevailed on your goodwill under false pretenses."

Startled, Faith didn't know how to respond.

"I wanted to talk to you about Emilie, the woman who died." Martha drew her brows together in a frown.

Oh no, not more questions, more gossip. Faith supposed it was only natural for Martha to want to know what happened. But the staff of Castleton Manor had worked hard to distract the retreat guests, to keep a lid on the awful details while the police discreetly went about their investigation. She hadn't suspected Martha as the nosy type, but here she was, wanting to talk about Emilie. "Mrs. Weathers—"

"Call me Martha. And please don't misunderstand. I taught for nearly forty years before retiring. Thirty years ago, when I was teaching elementary school in Providence, Emilie was one of my students. She was a brilliant child, but she was desperately unable to fit in with the other students. I wanted to help her but . . ."

Faith waited for her to continue.

Martha's eyes grew moist as she looked down memory's long passageway. "It was hard. Emilie was so secretive, so different from the other students. Her parents kept to themselves." She grimaced as if the memory was unpleasant. "Every blended family has difficulties, but Emilie was very troubled."

"We're terribly sorry for what happened to Emilie, but we don't know—"

"I'm not here to collect gossip, believe me," Martha interrupted, intuiting Faith's reluctance. "I just want to know what happened to her." She suddenly grew restive, shuffling her feet and crossing and uncrossing her arms. Then she stood, paced back and forth, and returned to her chair.

"Are you all right?" Faith asked, unsettled by this unusual behavior.

Martha opened a small purse that lay in her lap and tentatively removed a piece of paper. "I found this under my door. I think it must have come from Emilie." She held it out to Faith with a hand that wasn't altogether steady.

Faith read it slowly.

Good bye to the Life I used to live—
And the World I used to know—
And kiss the Hills, for me, just once—
Then—I am ready to go!

"It's part of a Dickinson poem," Martha said in a hushed voice.

"Yes. The last stanza of 'Farewell.'" Faith shivered. Was this the suicide note? Proof that Emilie had planned to kill herself? She searched Martha's eyes.

"I was getting ready for bed when I noticed it slipped under the door. I looked out into the hall, but I didn't see anyone. It was quite late. I couldn't imagine what it was. Oh, if I had known she was going to . . ." Martha sighed deeply. "Of course I recognized Emilie that first day when we arrived. I told her how good it was to see her, but she didn't seem to know me, or at least she didn't want to talk to me." She pressed her hands together, clearly upset. "But I couldn't have helped then. It was too late, wasn't it?"

"When was this? When did you find the note?"

"It was Wednesday night."

"Wednesday?" Faith repeated, her pulse picking up. "But she couldn't have. We found Emilie dead on Tuesday morning."

"I know." Martha waited a moment and then added in a shaky voice, "I received the note the night after Emilie died."

Faith's mind whirled as she tried to absorb this new information. If Emilie hadn't put the note there, then who had? The same person who had ransacked the Emily Dickinson Suite? And why? It made no sense at all. "Are you sure the note wasn't there the day before and you just didn't notice it?"

"I'm sure. I've heard the rumors that the police are looking into Emilie's death, that she might not have been alone that night. But this note sounds like—well, like she was saying goodbye."

Faith scrutinized the handwriting that appeared to be Emilie's. She imagined the paper had been torn from a notebook or a letter. "I don't know. But it must be shared with Chief Garris, and he will probably want to talk to you about it." *And perhaps to young Wilhelmina too,* she thought.

"Thank you," Martha said, lowering her voice. "I needed to discuss this with someone. I only wish I had known how troubled Emilie still was. Maybe I could have done something."

A thud came from behind Faith's desk where shelves of books stood as well as the rolling cart she used for restocking shelves.

Faith jumped, surprised, for only she and Martha were in the library as far as she knew. They exchanged confused looks.

"Excuse me." Faith set the note on her desk, then got up to investigate.

Two books lay on the floor. Apparently, they had been stacked too close to the edge and had fallen off the rolling cart. She glanced around for someone she hadn't known was present. The area was void of human but not animal habitation, for Watson scooted out from beneath the cart with a loud meow.

"Watson!" she scolded, scooping him up. "You've been doing your pouncing thing and look what you've done. And after you promised to be good."

Ears erect, Watson wiggled to be free. When he escaped her grasp and dropped to the floor, Faith noticed that his fur was standing straight up. Like most cats, Watson didn't like loud noises and sudden movement. He glanced around warily, whiskers alert, as if to say, "Was it something I did?"

Had Watson been chasing something? Maybe a mouse? Or had someone been here? Someone who had bumped into the cart in an attempt to get away? She tried to laugh off her nerves. That was silly. If someone had entered the library, she had simply not noticed. Or had someone been spying on them? Listening to their private conversation?

She bent to pick Watson up again, and this time he made no effort to free himself. She carried him back to her desk and smiled apologetically at Martha who stood there waiting. "I'm sorry for the interruption. This is my cat, Watson. He's very curious, and when he's in a playful mood he likes to pounce. He seems to have knocked some books off my rolling cart."

"He's a handsome fellow." Martha reached out to pet him. "And what a clever name."

"It suits him," Faith said. "There's nothing he likes better than investigating, like a feline Sherlock Holmes. Some folks call it snooping."

Martha smiled. "Well, I do appreciate your taking the time to see me. Lunch should be over now, and the library will be getting busy. I must say, I think this is the most elegant, most splendid of all the rooms here at the manor, and you have been a most gracious librarian."

They regarded each other briefly, suddenly serious.

Faith motioned to her desk where the scrap of paper with its ominous message still rested. "Do you want me to give the note to the police?"

"Oh, thank you," Martha said, her relief obvious.

"I'm sure the police will get to the bottom of this," Faith assured her. She offered a hand in farewell, and Martha grasped it readily.

When Martha was gone, Faith sat down wearily, holding Watson in her arms. His soft warmth was always comforting, but Martha's news lay heavily on her heart. And there was something niggling at the back of her mind. Even if Watson had pounced on the cart from a high shelf, the motion wasn't strong enough to dislodge books from the cart. Was it? Had someone indeed been listening?

"Well, Watson," she whispered, mystified, "this is one for the books."

The next few hours passed rapidly as retreat guests came to the library with their various requests. Faith hadn't forgotten her promise to look in on Carlo at the kennels. She relished the undemanding companionship of the animal world. She'd packed Carlo's treats along with her comfortable boots.

She snagged a few minutes when the library was empty to call Eileen. Faith told her about giving her statement to Chief Garris and asked her to turn Emilie's documents over to the police.

Eileen agreed and then added, "By the way, are you free to go fishing tomorrow?"

More than a little taken aback, Faith could only manage an unintelligent response. "Huh?"

Eileen went on as if she hadn't heard. "And we'll need some bait. So we'll have to stop at the shop near the docks."

Faith understood. "You mean the one owned by Bentley and Emilie Smythe's half sister, Maggie?"

"The very same."

Faith chuckled. "Sure, Aunt Eileen."

"See you then!" And her aunt was gone.

Faith was about to lock up for the afternoon when the door opened. Bentley Smythe, wearing chinos, a white cable-knit sweater, and a jacket slung carelessly over one shoulder, entered.

She drew in her breath, for the likeness to Emilie was so strong. That nearly black hair, eyes the color of obsidian, aristocratic nose and jaw. Faith had been puzzled by her attraction to him from their first meeting, yet something made her wary. If she could only be as confident and coy as Brooke, who was always at ease with a handsome suitor. *Suitor? I've been reading too much Victorian poetry.*

Watson jumped off her lap and sat alert, watching the newcomer from several feet away.

She greeted Bentley in what she hoped was an offhand manner.

"I'm glad I caught you. Things have been a little crazy around here, and I've had so many details to attend to . . ." Bentley's voice trailed off.

What details had kept Bentley occupied? Funeral plans? But the police were still holding the body as the investigation ramped up following the coroner's report. Or was he referring to details connected to his import-export business? She imagined the wealthy man's connections around the globe, his formidable successes, and the grand mansion he occupied. And yet death had a way of leveling the playing field. *It makes us all vulnerable*, she thought. It must be awful to know that someone close to you might have died at the hands of someone else.

Bentley remained silent as he searched her face. He had a way of looking through a person. Not in a leering sort of way but intrusive all the same.

"Are you all right?" she asked.

"It's kind of you to be concerned," he said. "I guess none of us will be all right until this thing is resolved."

This thing. Funny, the euphemisms people used for emotionally laden subjects. Faith wasn't sure what to say to that.

"I wondered if you would have dinner with me later tonight." Bentley's voice was as mellow as the grand library's ambience. "We could go to that new seafood restaurant in Lighthouse Bay. I've heard it's spectacular. Could you be available at eight o'clock?"

Her mind spun, first with surprise, then with all she'd learned about Emilie and all she still wanted to know. Here was her brother who might add to that knowledge. There was time to visit the kennels before dark and still be free by eight. Why not? She felt her ears tingle like they always did when she was anxious or delighted. "That would be nice," she heard herself say and wished she'd used anything but the banal word *nice*.

"I'll see you at eight, then," he said, tipping his head in a partial bow.

Faith had yet to learn the identity of the short man in jeans and a black nylon jacket who had stood with Bentley on the upper level before the poetry reading. Still unnerved by the sense that someone had been eavesdropping on her and Martha earlier, she decided to ask Bentley about him directly. "Did you enjoy the poetry reading last night?"

He raised an eyebrow. "I did, though I must say I don't go in for versification." He slipped on his jacket and buttoned it, obviously preparing to take his leave.

"And the fellow you were speaking with. I don't believe I met him."

"Oh? I thought he was one of your retreat guests," Bentley replied smoothly. "We exchanged a few words, and he left. Probably to take advantage of the refreshments being served downstairs. Why?"

She shrugged. "No reason. I was just curious."

"I must say, though I don't go in for poetry much, I thought your handling of the evening was excellent." He flashed her a brilliant smile. "I'll call for you at eight at your cottage." And he was gone, this time with a full-fledged bow.

12

Faith headed to the kennels with Watson frolicking alongside. A thin sun shone bravely, but the brisk wind penetrated her all-weather anorak. With this erratic April weather, the first lines of T. S. Eliot's poem "The Waste Land" sprang to her mind.

April is the cruellest month, breeding
Lilacs out of the dead land, mixing
Memory and desire, stirring
Dull roots with spring rain.

And this month is especially cruel. Its ground would soon receive a woman who died much too soon, who would never see another April dance across the stage on gossamer wings.

When they drew near the kennels, Watson raced ahead, no longer content to amble along beside Faith. She smiled. Watson, who usually put up with dogs as sorry facts of life, had discovered a friend in the Newfoundland. And Carlo had exhibited uncommon patience with the cat. He let out a deep-throated woof as Watson slipped through the metal bars and began batting at his thumping tail. Soon the two friends were chasing each other around the kennel.

"This big boy will be glad for some special TLC," Annie Jennings said, sidling up to Carlo's large kennel.

"Do you have a minute to talk?" Faith asked her.

"Sure," Annie said, tucking her hands, thumbs out, into the pockets of her jeans.

"I guess you've heard by now that the police are investigating Emilie's death as suspicious."

"Yeah, I know." Annie tossed her thick brown braid over her plaid shoulder and turned to watch Carlo and Watson playing. "Carlo was with her that night. The poor fella was pretty upset when Midge brought him back. But he's calmed down somewhat now, and we've been giving him all the attention we can." She sighed. "Too bad he can't talk. He may be the only one who knows what really happened out there."

Faith nodded. "Have the police been here to ask you what time Emilie picked Carlo up on Monday?"

"Officer Laddy stopped by. I told him that Miss Smythe came for him at about eight o'clock that night."

"Did she say where she was going or when she planned to bring Carlo back?"

"Nope. We keep records of the hours that pets spend here, but we're never sure what to expect. Sometimes guests keep their animals with them all the time in their rooms, but I guess that would be difficult with a dog as big as Carlo." Annie shrugged. "The rules don't usually allow for a pet his size. We never had a Newfie before."

Yes, Faith thought. *Special dispensation in Emilie's case. Had it been Wolfe's decision since he and Bentley had been buddies in college?* Yet she was surprised how seldom she'd seen the two together at Castleton. Nor had Wolfe given the impression that he was fond of his old friend.

"You have any idea what's going to happen to Carlo now?" Annie asked. "Is Miss Smythe's family coming to get him?"

Faith frowned. Bentley had made it clear that his lifestyle allowed no place for pet ownership. And who else would take Carlo? Maggie Haggedorn, the estranged half sister? It was sad to think Carlo might end up in a shelter, waiting for a home. What was the likelihood that the huge Newfie would be adopted? "I don't know, but it will be Mr. Smythe's decision."

Annie toyed thoughtfully with the bandanna around her neck. "It's odd, isn't it?"

"What?"

"If there had been someone out there on that ledge when Miss Smythe—" Annie floundered and tugged at her bandanna again. "Well, wouldn't Carlo have made a right noisy ruckus trying to defend his master? She was no sweetheart, but Carlo was very loyal to her. Newfies are known for that—loyal to a fault no matter how you treat them."

Faith had wondered the same thing. She couldn't imagine that Carlo had accidentally caused Emilie's fall as Officer Laddy had suggested. They had found Carlo next to Emilie, refusing to budge when the authorities tried to remove the body. If he had been there when Emilie was accosted, what could explain his apparent inaction? Had he tried to stop the attacker? Maybe there was someone walking around Lighthouse Bay with a Newfie-sized dog bite. Had the police checked with doctors or hospitals in the area?

"It's puzzling for sure," Faith agreed. "If you think of anything else, will you let me know?"

"You got it," Annie said. She pointed to Carlo and Watson tussling together. "Look at the two of them. Carlo really is a gentle old boy, and Watson seems to take to him. That doesn't always happen with cats and dogs."

Faith knelt to fondle Carlo's ears. He wriggled happily when she pulled a strawberry pup-tart from her jacket. "Here you go, boy."

He gobbled it down in one gulp as Watson watched demurely. Had the big dog even tasted it?

She patted his flank affectionately and was surprised when he yelped in pain. "What's wrong, buddy?"

"Oh, I forgot to mention that," Annie said. "Carlo's been reacting to something. He's got a little sore right there." She gently separated the fur so Faith could see it. "We put some salve on it, but it still seems tender."

Faith peered at the small red area. "What is it?"

"We're not sure. There was some dried blood around the spot, and we sponged it off. It doesn't seem to bother him unless you touch it, though."

"Does it have anything to do with the mange he's being treated for?" Faith would have liked a closer look, but Carlo was having none of it.

"I don't think so," Annie said. "It could be he tangled with a thornbush or something."

A little flag waved at the back of Faith's mind. "When did you first notice it?"

"Just this morning when I was brushing him," Annie replied. "Another attendant has been doing the grooming, but she hasn't said anything about it."

Faith made a mental note to talk to Midge. If that tender spot wasn't there before the day Emilie died, it might have something to do with what had happened to her. *I'm grasping at straws*, she thought. But there seemed to be nothing but straws here, intangible and imagined.

For now, she and Watson had better scoot. She had to drop off the note from Martha at the police station, and she had a few other things to do before Bentley came to pick her up, including finding something suitable to wear.

"I hope I'm not too early," Bentley said when Faith opened the front door. He wore the gray suit and chambray shirt she remembered from his first visit to the library, but he had added a charcoal cashmere overcoat and a white silk scarf. The porch light glistened on his dark hair. "These are for you." He held out a small bouquet of pink tulips.

Faith swallowed at the unexpected gesture. It had been some time since a man had bought her flowers. "Thank you. They're lovely. Won't you come in while I put them in some water?"

Bentley ducked his head to enter, though it wasn't necessary. It was probably a reflex action most tall men employed. "This is a charming cottage." He moved into the center of the living room, appearing restive.

Watson followed Faith to the kitchen but stopped in the doorway, then sat down and began washing his face with his paws. The cat remained intent on the visitor who was browsing the living room with what seemed like overly studied attention. This time, Faith realized, Watson hadn't run off as he had when Bentley came to the library. But he was clearly not a fan. She gave her preening pet a cautionary glance and hoped he would behave himself.

"I heard this was once a humble gardener's cottage," Bentley said when she had returned and picked up her coat from the back of the couch. "It's elegant but cozy."

A humble gardener's cottage. The comment rankled briefly, but perhaps she was too sensitive. After all, her home was just that. "Thanks," she said simply.

The Captain's Table proved to be everything it was rumored to be, an upscale restaurant within sight of the historic lighthouse with pristine white tablecloths, gleaming china, and fine silver. Faith ordered a Roquefort pear salad, followed by steak and lobster with garlic-and-chimichurri butter and rolls so soft they melted in her mouth.

Bentley similarly chose the steak and lobster with a spinach salad. "I'm glad you agreed to dinner tonight. I've been wanting to get to know you better."

Faith wondered why a successful international export dealer who likely had contacts in every corner of the globe would be interested in a simple librarian. *You always sell yourself short*, Brooke often said. Perhaps she did. Still, Bentley's intrusive manner intimidated her. "So, you travel all over the world in your export business?" she asked, adroitly placing her knife crosswise on her plate.

He nodded. "It becomes more and more important in our technologically advanced environment. We've really shifted toward one-world modes of thought."

"It's always seemed rather mysterious to me," Faith confessed.

"The history of international trade can be traced to the great caravans of long ago with their cargoes of silks and spices, even back to prehistoric man trading shells and salt with distant tribes." Bentley's dark eyes grew animated. "One group or country has a supply of some commodity or merchandise that's in demand by another. Simple as that." He held out his hands, palms up.

"It must have been lonely for Emilie when you were away," Faith said. She wasn't very interested in his business, but she was eager to learn more about his relationship with other members of the family.

"She wasn't alone. Our housekeeper is more than a domestic. She's become part of the family, and Emilie was fond of her. Besides, Emilie traveled a great deal on her own, both in the States and abroad. She had her studies and her writing. She was very talented and moved in intercollegiate circles, and she often lectured on literary matters."

"Really?" Faith said. "And when did her profound interest in Dickinson begin?"

"Quite early. She was overly fixated on the Smythe family history," he said nonchalantly. "She combined facts with imaginative leanings, and it got to be all she thought about."

"I guess that's why she dressed like the poet and even adopted a dog like Emily Dickinson's. I must say, I've grown rather fond of Carlo. And Watson has claimed him as a comrade in arms—or should I say paws."

Bentley exhaled a slow breath as though resigned to his sister's strange behavior.

"How did your sister Margaret get along with Emilie?" Faith asked, pressing further. She wondered what he would think if she told him that she had agreed to go fishing with Aunt Eileen tomorrow and planned to patronize the bait and tackle shop run by Maggie Haggedorn. Faith hoped the woman could shed some light on what had happened to Emilie. "I know they were several years apart in age."

"Ten years, to be exact. I think I told you before that Margaret is my half sister. After Margaret's mother died, Father remarried and then Emilie and I were born." He set his coffee cup down with precision. "Margaret never accepted my mother. She always claimed her birth mother was perfect and that our father was duped into an unsatisfactory second marriage." The shrug that followed seemed a gesture of resignation.

Faith recalled Aunt Eileen describing Maggie as the forgotten stepdaughter and the black sheep of the Smythe family.

"Margaret left one day and never looked back. I believe she was briefly married to a fisherman from Wales who was killed in an accident at sea."

"That's so sad," Faith said, imagining the bereaved woman living out her life close to the sea where her husband had died and not knowing—or refusing—the comfort of family. Bitterness could very well overtake her. "I'm sorry to hear it."

"We all make our choices," he said simply. "Saints and sinners alike." Faith thought she saw a glint of regret in Bentley's eyes.

Faith considered his strange words. Something about his reference to saints was nagging at the back of her mind. A long moment of silence followed as she thought back. There was something about saints in one of the documents Emilie had given her. Yes, that scrap of paper mixed in with the yellowed pages that mentioned meeting at the lighthouse.

> *The lighthouse at ten.*
> *Prithee don't fail me.*
> *The saints are watching—*
> *anon they hail thee.*

It would soon be time to pay a visit to Maggie Haggedorn. What had the police deduced about her? They had certainly questioned her as well as Bentley's housekeeper and anyone else who had known Emilie.

A chill rode up her spine. Was it possible that Maggie had killed her half sister out of revenge or some misguided sense of devotion? Suddenly, Faith remembered the fishing lure she'd removed from Watson's fur the day they'd found Emilie. Had it come from Maggie's bait and tackle shop?

Curled up by the fire, the cat listened for the sound of his human, who should have been home by now. He was eager for his bedtime snack and some cuddle time. He engaged in these evening activities condescendingly. After all, it wouldn't do for a self-respecting cat to seem too anxious. But she was late, and his stomach told him supper had been a long time ago. He roused himself and sprang onto the back of the couch to watch for her.

A human was coming, but it wasn't her. This one was walking—or rather skulking, as though not wanting to be seen. The shadowy form didn't stop at the door. It went around the side and peered in the window.

He climbed down from the couch and padded into the kitchen. His sharp ears heard the footsteps, then the creaking sound of the pantry window. A human was coming, a stranger. As much as he hated to admit it, his hackles were quivering. He didn't trust strangers.

He crouched, then leaped up onto the table and from there to the top of the refrigerator. He peeked into the pantry from his mountaintop. The intruder was inside and about to step into the kitchen. His human wouldn't like this at all.

It was up to him now. With his grandest hiss, he jumped on the intruder's head.

"Dinner was wonderful. Thank you," Faith said when they returned to her cottage. She ought to ask Bentley in for coffee. It was the polite thing to do, but something made her hesitate on the stone step. Besides, it was late and she was tired. She touched his arm. "Good night, Bentley. I hope this will all be settled soon, so you and your family will find closure."

He seemed disinclined to leave, but after a few awkward seconds he said, "Thanks for a great evening."

After waving farewell, she turned the key in the lock . . . and instantly felt the hairs on the back of her neck tingle.

There was no need for a key. Had she forgotten to lock the front door? She should call Bentley back, but she felt frozen on the threshold. Faith listened. Quiet reigned, except for the soft susurration of ocean waves—a sound she usually loved, especially at night as she awaited sleep. How many times had she come and gone from this cottage? She'd never felt the sense of another's presence as she did now.

Where was Watson, who usually came to greet her? Faith called him—softly at first, then more urgently. The automatically timed lamp by the sofa revealed no intruder. Everything in the living room looked exactly as she'd left it. The desk's smooth surface was clean of paper or debris, the stapler poised just so, the pencil caddy unmoved. Nothing seemed disturbed in her bedroom either—the bureau, the closet, her jewelry box. The drawers didn't appear to have been rifled through. Nothing seemed to be missing.

Was her imagination running away with her? She felt for the comfortable lump of her cell phone against her thigh and went into the kitchen. What was that odd smell? "Watson? Watson! Where are you?" Her voice echoed through the room to the steady *ticktock* of the wall clock.

A high-pitched meow issued from somewhere above her.

"Watson?"

And there he was on top of the refrigerator, eyes wide and watchful. *Whoosh!* The soft pads of his feet hit the floor, and he twined himself agitatedly against her ankles.

Faith bent to gather him up, but he swerved out of her grasp and darted past her into the living room. She followed him there, then to the bedroom and to the bath. Watson inspected the house as though it was new to him and every corner must be explored.

Why was he acting so strangely? Had he been surprised by a noise? Perhaps someone knocking on the door or the shutters flapping in the wind? He liked to pounce, but she'd never known him to leap as high as the refrigerator. At his low, unsettled meow, she reached down to pick him up. Faith stroked his back and shoulders and felt his rapid heartbeat before he squirmed to get down and padded back into the kitchen. She followed him into the pantry, then drew in a sharp breath.

Cold air swept through the small room's only window, which was raised a few inches. Someone must have broken in there and failed to shut it all the way after passing through. She shivered. *Think!*

She hadn't noticed any of her valuables or other belongings missing or even out of place. There was nothing else for anyone to find. The letters and documents were all safe in police custody, but then, that wasn't widely known. Were those documents, bogus or not, the reason for the break-in? Obviously, someone who believed they were genuine had searched the Emily Dickinson Suite at Castleton Manor. The same someone might have learned that Emilie had given them to the manor's librarian.

Remembering the beaded bag, Faith dashed into the living room to pry loose the fireplace brick. The bag was still there. It was empty, for she'd taken the documents to Candle House and Eileen had turned them over to the police. She tossed the bag aside, not caring where it landed, replaced the brick, and went back into the kitchen where that strange scent once more struck her. Something minty like strong cough drops or . . . menthol?

Faith had smelled that odor before. Wilhelmina! The sullen young woman who had spoken of Emilie with such contempt. Disbelief and anger welled inside her. The nerve of her to invade Faith's personal space! But Wilhelmina hadn't reckoned on a feline attack. Watson had probably pounced from atop the refrigerator and sent Wilhelmina fleeing out the front door, which was why it had been unlocked. It couldn't have been too long ago, since the intruder's scent was still detectable.

If Wilhelmina Hodge had indeed been the intruder, she was most likely sporting a Watson-sized scratch somewhere on her scrawny body.

13

"Why, aren't you the early bird," Marlene remarked as Faith entered the dining room at Castleton Manor. Trim and elegant in a lavender suit with a long tunic, she stood at the antique walnut buffet that held refreshments and sipped at a cup of coffee. "So, what are you doing here?"

Ever the sweet voice of welcome. Faith groaned inwardly but met the assistant manager's scrutiny with a pleasant smile. "Looking for you, actually," she said while scanning the room. She spotted some familiar faces in the smattering of guests but not the one she was searching for. Maybe Wilhelmina was breakfasting in her room. Was that because of her natural antisocial tendencies, or was she shunning company after last night's nocturnal foray into Faith's cottage?

Faith had had a hard time getting to sleep after discovering the open window in her pantry. Even the soothing sounds of the surf hadn't worked their magic. Had she neglected to lock up before heading out with Bentley for dinner? Had she only imagined the odor of menthol, or had Wilhelmina truly been in her house? Should she have immediately called the police and had them dust for fingerprints?

But a thorough search of the cottage had revealed nothing missing or disturbed. Except Watson, of course, who'd clearly behaved in an unusual manner. She'd finally slept with him curled at her feet, but only after she'd determined to confront the suspect the very next morning. Saturday would be a good time, for retreat guests had recreational activities scheduled.

"Do you have a minute?" Faith asked, gesturing to a circular group of chairs in a quiet corner at the back of the room.

"It sounds serious," Marlene intoned in her imperious fashion as they walked over to the seating area. "Mr. Cat under the weather?"

Faith bit back a retort. Marlene's sensitivity, or lack thereof, was truly amazing sometimes. She sat down across from her and cleared her throat. "Nothing like that. This is important, and I need to ask your help."

Marlene raised her brows. She put her cup down on the end table and waited, curiosity sparking in her eyes.

"Someone broke into my cottage last night," Faith blurted out, then paused a few seconds before continuing. "I had a dinner engagement, and when I returned I discovered my front door unlocked and the window in the pantry open."

"Keep your voice down. We don't want the guests to overhear." Marlene glanced around before asking, "Was anything taken? Did they break something?"

"No, nothing was disturbed or taken, but someone had been in there."

Marlene frowned and released a long, drawn-out breath. "Are you sure you didn't just forget to lock the door?"

"I'm sure." *Well, 99 percent sure,* she thought. "The pantry window was raised, and cold air was streaming in. I think someone came in through that window. Also, there was this lingering smell . . ." She let the words trail off at Marlene's dubious expression.

"Look," Marlene said, folding her arms over her chest, "everyone has been on edge since Miss Smythe's death. It's not hard to imagine all manner of things."

"Did you imagine what happened to the Dickinson suite?" Faith challenged. "I believe someone is looking for those documents Emilie bragged about. I think they ransacked the Dickinson suite, then searched my cottage. Those documents would be worth a fortune if they're proved genuine. We don't think they are, but the police are bringing in expert analysts from Boston to check them over thoroughly."

Marlene paled slightly. "This whole thing has been a nightmare.

I wish our police department would get a move on and clear it all up." She released another exasperated breath. "So, you said you need my help? How exactly?"

"I know you've tried to distract the guests from anything to do with the Emilie Smythe investigation—"

"And it hasn't been easy," Marlene interrupted.

"I'd like you to make an announcement to everyone here at the retreat," Faith went on, undaunted. "Something to clearly indicate that Emilie's personal effects, including the documents that claim relationship to the great poet, have been turned over to the police. As long as someone thinks those documents are here at Castleton, in the library, or in the possession of the librarian, there could be more trouble."

"If there's anything we don't want, it's any more trouble over that ridiculous claim of hers." Marlene tightened her jaw. "All right, I'll make the announcement at dinner."

"I knew I could count on you," Faith said. "By the way, have you seen Wilhelmina Hodge today?"

"Ah yes, Wilhelmina. The social misfit joined at the hip to Martha Weathers." Marlene cringed at her own less-than-charitable comment. "I believe she was convinced to go horseback riding with the group." She narrowed her eyes. "What do you want with her?"

Faith searched her mind for a reasonable explanation to seek out Wilhelmina. "I just want to talk to her about her poem at the reading the other night. It would resonate with the work of Roethke. I thought I'd suggest she study it." Theodore Roethke's poem "My Papa's Waltz" had indeed occurred to Faith during the young woman's reading.

Marlene picked up her coffee and stood, obviously ready to move on with her day. She shrugged. "They'll be back later today."

"You won't forget about the announcement?" Faith asked as Marlene walked off.

She glanced back with an annoyed expression. "They don't pay me to forget," she said with considerable scorn and strode away.

Faith stopped at her cottage to pick up a warmer jacket and her comfortable boots. She had hoped to find Wilhelmina at the manor, but she would enjoy a walk to the stables, which would also afford an opportunity to look in on Carlo, maybe even take him along for the day's fishing adventure.

"You game?" she asked Watson, who had been watching for her return from his perch on the back of the sofa.

He jumped down and trotted to the door, whiskers alert.

It was still cool as they set out, but a brave sun gentled the brisk wind. Faith's mind whirled with thoughts and half thoughts, most of them centered on the disturbing death of the Dickinson look-alike. Was it all an unfortunate accident? The note with the chilling poem that alluded to leaving this world had mysteriously turned up under Martha's door but only after Emilie's body had been found. Who had put it there and why? Or was Martha mistaken about when she'd received it?

Had someone pushed Emilie to her death? Someone angry enough to leave bruises behind? Faith, Midge, and Brooke had seen Devon Hamlin in close proximity to the scene. The police had questioned Devon at length, exploring any possible connection to Emilie, yet they hadn't established a motive or uncovered any damaging evidence.

Still, Devon had behaved strangely by leaving the retreat early, and what was that black eye all about when she and Midge had visited his shop? Faith was certain that Devon had been involved in some sort of ruckus that he didn't want the police to know about. But it was only natural that he didn't want further attention drawn to his affairs.

Her mind turned to the handsome Bentley. She knew that a family member was nearly always the first suspect in an investigation. Family tensions could escalate to the point of murder. But Bentley hadn't even been in the country when Emilie died, and Faith had been touched by his pain, reaching out with what comfort she could give.

And then there was Maggie Haggedorn, the estranged and probably resentful half sister. Faith felt in her anorak pocket for the fishing lure she had pulled from Watson's fur the day they'd found Emilie's body. Had it come from Maggie's bait and tackle shop? Faith hoped they would soon find out. She had arranged for Aunt Eileen to pick her up at the manor in an hour for their little fishing trip and visit to Maggie's shop.

Faith wasn't much of a fisherman, but Eileen was always eager to catch some of the first bass of the season. She said most of those caught in the early spring were "micro-schoolies"—less than twenty inches long—and didn't require a great deal of gear or effort. Faith sighed. The only fish she was interested in snagging at the moment walked on two feet and was causing havoc at her beloved Castleton Manor.

As Faith approached the stables, she saw the group of riders returning with Samuel Peak at the lead, his unmistakable white mustache glistening in the sun. Two lengths behind the manor's head groom was Wilhelmina Hodge on a strawberry roan. Her gaze was fixed on the ground as the horse plodded into the corral. Did that long hair over her face hide a telling scratch?

Faith waited by the gate for the group to dismount, knowing the young woman would have no choice but to walk past her. She gathered Watson up in her arms. "Hello, Wilhelmina."

The young woman lifted her head, revealing a face wreathed in surprise that quickly turned ashen. Red acne blotches flared on her cheeks and above her dark eyebrows. Her mouth opened, but no words emerged.

"Enjoy your ride?" Faith persisted, tightening her grip on a wriggling Watson.

A low sound that was not a purr rattled in the cat's throat. If she needed more confirmation that her assessment about the break-in was correct, she had it. Watson remembered the intruder, and he wasn't a happy camper. He squirmed from her grip and leaped to the ground. Ignoring a quivering Wilhelmina, he headed off toward the kennels, no doubt to seek the more amiable company of other animals.

Wilhelmina jumped back as though expecting to be attacked. "I—what are you doing here?" she croaked.

"We were looking for you," Faith said, holding her gaze steadily. "I thought there might be something you wanted to tell me."

Wilhelmina shivered in her fleece jacket and said nothing for several seconds. When she spoke, shame seemed to swallow her words. "You know, don't you?" she said miserably. "I'm sorry."

"You broke into my cottage, and all you can say is you're sorry?" Faith retorted.

Wilhelmina's shoulders drooped, and her whole body seemed to sag. Then she broke into sobs.

Repentant? Or putting on an act? Faith stood her ground, though everything within her wanted to give comfort. Wilhelmina was no child, yet there was something terribly vulnerable about her. Faith gestured to a rough-hewn log bench. "Do you want to sit down?" she asked evenly.

Wilhelmina moved to the bench and sat, clasping her hands and resting them in her blue-jeaned lap. "I didn't plan to do it. I was just walking, and I saw your cottage there. I noticed the pantry window open a little, and I was going to squeeze in, take the letters, and get out. I thought—" She broke off and put a hand to her mouth. "The talk is that you have the letters about Emily Dickinson. I wanted the gossip about her and that married man to stop. I wanted to burn the letters."

"I don't understand you at all," Faith said in a rush. "Even if you could stop people from talking—which you can't—what you did makes no sense. You broke the law! Emily Dickinson is long dead, and her prodigious work has only enhanced her memory in the hearts of millions. Can the few who speculate about her personal life really hurt her?" She let out her breath in a frustrated sigh. "At least Watson stopped you from tearing up the place like you did to the beautiful Dickinson suite."

"But I didn't do that!" Wilhelmina protested, shaking her head vehemently. "I didn't! It wasn't me, I swear. I only looked in your cottage." She began to sob again, more loudly this time.

Once more Faith resisted the urge to put a comforting arm around Wilhelmina's shaking shoulders. Whoever had ransacked the Dickinson suite had left behind no fingerprints or other evidence. She no longer believed the shy young woman had ransacked that suite, but all the same, it would have been wise for Faith to call the police right away and have the pantry window dusted for prints. "For heaven's sake, why would you do something so"—she stopped herself from saying the word *stupid* or *bizarre*—"extreme?"

"When are they going to arrest me?" she asked through hiccuping sobs.

"I haven't informed the authorities—yet," Faith said, keeping the sternness in her voice. "I wanted to give you a chance to explain."

"I-I'm so sorry. It was stupid, and your cat had every right to scratch my eyes out. But he just thumped down on my head. He didn't even have his claws out."

Faith couldn't suppress a bubble of humor pressing its way to the surface. "No scratches then?"

"No, but he scared me half to death. I ran out your front door." After a few seconds, Wilhelmina knit her brow. "I deserve to be arrested. I don't know why you're being so kind to me. Nobody is—well, except for Mrs. Weathers." She bit her lip hard enough that a thin drop of blood appeared.

Faith waited, sensing the young woman had more to say.

"I don't want Emily Dickinson's name to suffer like my father's did." She narrowed her eyes. "After those vicious lies came out, I never saw him again, except for that one Christmas night when everyone was asleep and he brought the kitten to my bed." A tiny smile started, then slipped away.

Faith remembered some lines from the poem Wilhelmina had read a few nights earlier.

I hugged the little kitten—hugged it 'til it cried,
And I cried with childish passion
And longed for him instead.

"He was shamed all over town," Wilhelmina said more quietly. "Even my mother believed the things they said about him. How he'd gotten a woman in our small town pregnant. My mom turned him out of our house and had the court issue a restraining order." Her voice grew smaller and smaller until it was only a whisper. "It was a lie. They were all lies. But he lost everything—his family, his business, and his good name—and it ruined him. He killed himself the year I turned twelve."

What angst could invade a young girl's heart! And this time, Faith did put her arms around Wilhelmina and felt the thin body quiver against hers. She held her that way for several seconds until Wilhelmina drew back.

Faith removed a tissue from her jacket pocket and held it out to her. "I'm sorry too—sorry for what you had to go through as a child. But an unburied past will return to haunt you, to cause grief over and over again. The truth will prevail, both in your father's case and in Miss Dickinson's. You can be sure that one day it will be so."

Wilhelmina lifted her tearstained face. "I promise I won't cause any more trouble," she whispered.

"I believe you," Faith said, smiling encouragement. She checked her watch. "My aunt is coming soon. We can drop you back at the manor if you like."

"Thanks but I'll walk. It helps me to think." Wilhelmina stood, tucking her hands into the pockets of her fleece jacket, and gave Faith a lingering look as though she wanted to say more. But she only nodded slowly and walked away.

14

Eileen rumbled up the road in her old GMC pickup, which she had held on to even after purchasing a new Ford Mustang Coupe, and careened to a stop. She looked nothing like a librarian in her worn patchwork jacket and floppy camouflage hat. "Going my way?" she inquired, tossing her hair over her shoulder and winking at her niece.

"You know it," Faith called and swung herself up into the passenger seat. No one could lift her mood more quickly than her adventurous aunt Eileen. "Mind if we stop by the kennels and pick up Watson? He's visiting Carlo. I'd like to bring him along. Carlo, too, if that's okay with you."

"Sure, but with all that black hair, guest accommodations are in the rear."

Faith grinned. "I don't think he'd have it any other way."

"We'll roll out the tarp so he won't slip around back there." Aunt Eileen reached out and squeezed Faith's arm. "You doing all right, honey?" She had an uncanny ability to ferret out information or detect a mood.

"I think so." Faith looked out the window and spied Wilhelmina trudging back to the manor.

"One of the guests?" Eileen asked, following her gaze.

"Yes," Faith said. "Wilhelmina Hodge, the one who climbed in my pantry window last night."

"What?" The pickup lurched.

"It's all right," Faith said. "Watson scared her off."

"Three cheers for Watson! But why would that young woman break into your cottage?"

"She was looking for the Dickinson documents. But of course they weren't there anyway. She said she was going to take them and burn them. It was the strangest, saddest thing I ever heard."

Eileen pulled up by the kennels and put the truck in park. "Why would she do such a thing?"

"Wilhelmina's a huge fan of the famous poet, but that's only half the story. The other half concerns her father, who fell victim to vicious lies. After he lost everything, he took his own life. Wilhelmina didn't want Dickinson's name sullied like her father's was. She took the gossip about Dickinson quite personally and decided to do something about it."

Eileen's face paled. "She didn't kill Emilie, did she?"

"No, she wasn't responsible for Emilie's death, and I'm pretty sure she didn't ransack the Dickinson suite either. Whoever searched it was a pro. Wilhelmina didn't even try to cover her tracks. I doubt it even occurred to her." Faith filled in the details as they spread out the tarp and loaded Carlo into the back of the pickup.

Watson climbed inside but watched Carlo through the glass from his vantage point on Faith's shoulder.

"I'm so glad you got those documents out of your cottage," Eileen said, continuing the conversation as they headed toward the wharf. "I hope everyone at the retreat knows the police have them now."

"Marlene agreed to make a special announcement just in case someone still thinks they're around here," Faith said. "They'd be worth a lot of money if they were proven to have merit."

"Some people will do anything for money." Eileen sighed deeply.

"At least Wilhelmina did what she did because she cared about a poet whose reputation might be damaged."

"So we're still in the dark about what really happened to Emilie out there on the rocks," Eileen remarked.

"We are," Faith confirmed. "And if the police are any nearer to making an arrest, I haven't heard about it."

"I wonder if they suspect Maggie Haggedorn."

"I'm sure they're not discounting anyone at this point. Do you think Maggie stands to gain something from Emilie's death?"

"I don't know since Maggie was already left out of the family inheritance. But close relatives are most often guilty in cases like these." Eileen glanced at Faith. "Speaking of relatives, I heard you and Bentley Smythe visited the new seaside restaurant."

Faith couldn't hide her surprise. "How did you know?"

Eileen laughed. "I'm sorry, honey. A friend of mine just started working there, and she mentioned seeing you. I didn't mean to pry."

"Oh, it's all right," Faith said, feeling her cheeks grow warm. Aunt Eileen was nearly as bad as Brooke when it came to trying to match her up with an eligible bachelor, though she made no bones about her preference for Wolfe. "Bentley's been staying at Castleton Manor, and we've talked a couple of times. He's . . ." She shrugged.

"Handsome and rich." Eileen grinned, then grew serious. "But what do you really know about him? You can't be too careful, you know."

Did Aunt Eileen actually believe Bentley could have had something to do with his sister's death? He hadn't been anywhere near Castleton Manor the night it happened. She recalled his ashen face and crumpled posture whenever he talked about Emilie. Besides, he was her brother.

"I don't usually pass along gossip," Eileen said slowly, "but I remember some years ago there was talk about Bentley's export business. It was something about artifacts brought into the country illegally. There was an investigation, but nothing came of it." She stopped a few yards from the wharf and set the brake.

Faith stared at her aunt, surprised at the news and at her own sense of quick indignation. People were always willing to expect the worst of the wealthy. Still, Eileen was right. No one should be overlooked until the facts of Emilie's death were uncovered. She swallowed her anxiety. There was still Maggie to be reckoned with.

"Come on. Carlo's getting antsy back there. We don't want him jumping out and running off." Faith took his leash from her bag and opened the truck door.

Watson jumped out before her feet touched the ground and danced around Carlo as Faith hooked up the dog's leash.

Aunt Eileen grabbed the poles and gear, and they all headed toward the little shack that housed the bait shop. Two elderly men fished at the end of the pier, and out on the water a canoe drifted some distance from shore. The scene was idyllic, a stunning vista an artist would yearn to paint.

What would it be like, Faith wondered, *to spend your days surrounded by water, doling out bait and fishing paraphernalia to vacationers and local patrons?*

Suddenly, Maggie Haggedorn stomped onto the front porch of the shack, her red-gray hair looking wild. The overalls Faith remembered seeing the day she and Aunt Eileen were having lunch at Snickerdoodles had been replaced by cuffed jeans and a baggy pea-green sweater. A bright bobber and a turquoise lure dangled from her worn leather vest.

"There she is," Faith said. "She looks upset. I wonder what's wrong."

"With Maggie, there's always something," Eileen replied.

Maggie's stormy gaze roamed the area as though she'd lost something and expected to find it in the blustery wind. She glared out over the pier where the old men fished, then at Faith and Eileen as they came toward her.

The two women wore fishing gear, with poles slung over their shoulders and Carlo loping along beside them on his leash. Faith had deliberately brought the dog along to see how he would react to Maggie, but he seemed unperturbed and wagged his tail happily as they approached. Watson stepped daintily along the pebbly path to the pier, his stub of a tail bouncing as he went.

As quickly as she'd appeared on the porch, Maggie vanished into the bait shop.

Faith and Eileen continued toward the shack, climbed the short wooden steps, and opened the screen door. They were instantly aware of a stuffy untidiness, of shelves upended and contents spilled onto the floor. A curtain dividing the store from what were probably living quarters was torn from its rod. Had someone vandalized the shop? Or was Maggie simply a messy shopkeeper?

Maggie, red-faced and grim, stood behind the counter. "Come back to finish what you started?" There was a flash of metal as she retrieved something from beneath the counter. A shotgun!

Astonished and perplexed, Faith stood stock-still.

"It won't be so easy this time!" Maggie shouted. "I'm here, and I know how to use this!"

At Faith's side, Carlo froze, his tail dropping to the floor like a fallen flag. A low growl came from his throat.

Faith's pulse raced. Carlo hadn't reacted to seeing Maggie, but the appearance of the gun had immediately made his hackles rise. She gripped his leash, feeling the blood drain from her face.

Maggie's ruddy complexion grew even redder. The gun trembled in her hand. "Someone thin and quick was running south along the shore. Could have been one of you. And now you've come back!"

The accusation was ludicrous. If Faith and Eileen had been here moments earlier, attempting to rob her, they would hardly return to the scene of the crime, even if they could double back that fast.

"Maggie, it's me, Eileen Piper from the Candle House Library." She didn't move but stood calmly, her voice soothing and low. "Are you all right?"

With a groan, Maggie put the gun down, apparently realizing that her accusation had no merit. She pushed back a lock of hair, which Faith saw was thick and curly and might have been beautiful once.

Carlo stopped growling, sat back on his haunches, and whimpered slightly.

Maggie pressed both hands against her temples, and Faith could see unshed tears glistening in her green eyes. "I left for half an hour to bury Dakota," she murmured, her voice cracking, "and I come back to this. Some thief all dressed in black, the coward!"

"I'm so sorry," Eileen said, picking up two cardboard cartons lying haphazardly at her feet. "Have you called the police?"

"No. No police. I don't want them swarming around again." Maggie clumped around the counter and stooped to retrieve a tray of lures that had toppled from a shelf. She replaced the rubbery green lures into their grooves, arranging them gingerly to avoid the sharp hooks attached. They wiggled like jelly in Maggie's fingers, as if they were alive.

Faith examined the lures. They had blue fins and a stark black eye painted artfully in the rubber and were exactly like the one she had removed from Watson's hindquarters the day they'd found Emilie. "Those lures are lovely," she said, stepping forward. "I'm Faith Newberry, by the way. Eileen is my aunt."

"They're nothing like the cheap ones Nathan's Fishing Supply sends me," Maggie said, ignoring the introduction. "I make those myself. Ten bucks apiece and worth every penny." She fixed Faith with a wary eye, then scowled at Carlo as though seeing the big Newfie for the first time. "What's that dog doing in here? Put him out." Her voice lacked malice, and Carlo didn't appear offended. "You can use the stake next to the porch." After a few seconds, she added, "Dakota won't need it no more."

Obediently, Faith urged Carlo to the door. She hooked his leash to the metal stake, relieved on two counts—that the Dakota Maggie had buried must have been her dog and that the irritable shopkeeper couldn't be all bad if she was fond of animals.

"Now, what is it you two want?" she demanded when Faith stepped back inside.

Eileen pressed forward. "We'd like to talk to you—"

"Talk? Talk about what?" She glanced from Eileen to Faith, eyes flashing with suspicion. "Wait a minute. Aren't you—?"

"I'm the librarian at Castleton Manor," Faith stated, holding Maggie's penetrating stare. "I'm the one who found your half sister. I want you to know how sorry I am for your loss. Everyone at Castleton Manor is saddened, and if there's anything we can do to help, please let us know."

Maggie crossed her arms over her chest and narrowed her eyes. "Well, if you know who I am, then you know I got nothing to do with Miss Emilie." Sarcasm dripped from her lips.

Faith tried hard to keep her anger in check. How was it that a sister, even a half sister, didn't appear to grieve over an untimely, senseless death and demand to know why? "I thought you might be able to relate something that would help us understand what happened to her."

"I told the police everything. There ain't nothing else to say, as if it's any of your business," Maggie spat.

"Everything?" Eileen piped up. "Do they know about that shotgun?"

"I keep it for protection, and I got a license."

"Did you explain to the police what this was doing just a few feet away from Emilie's body?" Faith pulled the scarf from her pocket and unwrapped it slowly, revealing the fishing lure.

Maggie didn't say a word, but her face lost its deep color and became almost ashen.

"It was found in a place where no one goes to fish. It's one of your handmade lures, isn't it?" Faith thrust it closer to Maggie's face.

"I sell them in my shop," Maggie said evenly, though her voice dropped to a whispered rasp. "Anyone could have left it there. If it *was* there," she sputtered. "You could have picked it up anywhere. Besides, the police never asked me about it." She reached for the lure.

But Faith yanked it away. "You and your sister didn't get along, did you?" she continued. She could hardly believe her own temerity. "Did you resent her and maybe Bentley too when you were excluded from the will?"

"What right do you have to barge in here and start accusing me?" Maggie railed, aghast. She stormed back around the counter, and for a moment, Faith thought the gun might make a second appearance. Instead, Maggie leaned against the counter, bracing herself with large, weathered hands. "For the record, the family estate was settled long ago, and I never wanted nothing from them."

Faith wondered if Maggie's abuse of the English language had been a bone of contention in the well-educated Smythe family. Perhaps she'd developed her folksy vernacular out of spite.

"I wasn't ever one of them—not after my mother died and *she* turned Daddy's head to mush."

Faith assumed Maggie was referring to her stepmother, Lillian. She glanced at her aunt, remembering: *Lillian liked to flaunt her wealth and had her husband bowing to her every whim. She saw that her two children had the best of everything, and in the end they were left a fortune.* Maggie, the stepdaughter, had been excluded. Had resentment built up to the point that she could have pushed Emilie from that cliff?

Maggie said bitterly, "They were never my family. All they wanted from me was someone to look after Emilie. 'See that Emilie doesn't wander off. Make sure Emilie drinks her milk.' She was nothing but trouble then. Now she's dead, and she's still causing me grief."

Faith drew in her breath. *Grief* was an interesting choice of words. Maggie didn't seem to be grieving, and apparently she hadn't had anything to do with her estranged family for years. It was all so tragic, so broken.

Maggie pushed away from the counter. "Now you can just get out of here," she blurted.

"We didn't mean to cause any trouble," Faith said quietly. "We only wanted to get at the truth. To know what happened to Emilie. Don't *you* want to know?"

"She jumped off the cliff. She finally gave up all that nonsense about our famous ancestor, her sick fascination, and running all over the country doing Bentley's bidding," Maggie sneered. "That's all the explanation I need."

What did she mean by "doing his bidding"? Faith pushed aside the question clamoring for an answer. "But the police don't believe she jumped. Someone was out there with her. Didn't they tell you there were bruises on her body?"

Maggie clamped her mouth shut, then clutched her stomach. After several seconds of silence, she gave Faith a disdainful look. "I don't have to talk to you. Go away!"

"I'm sorry," Faith said simply. "We're both sorry. We only want to know what happened."

"Come on," Eileen said, taking Faith's arm.

"Not until I find Watson," Faith objected. "My cat," she informed the glowering Maggie. "He's around here someplace." She called his name and peered behind counters and under shelves, where she knew he'd been exploring. Watson was the quintessential curious cat. When he didn't respond to her entreaties, Faith pointed to the torn curtain. "He's probably gone in the back."

Maggie pushed aside the curtain, muttering under her breath about her private quarters being invaded, especially when Faith followed her into the disordered back room.

"Come on out, Watson," Faith called, peeking under the bed. "Time to go home. Carlo's waiting for us."

But even the mention of his canine buddy stirred no response.

Faith walked around to the other side of the bed, where a lamp and clumps of newspaper had spilled onto the floor. And there was Watson, sitting sedately as though waiting for her to find him. She picked him up and looked down at what he'd been sitting on.

A cracked frame, out of which two faces emerged—one of a red-haired girl of sixteen or so, her arm wrapped protectively around a child with large dark eyes and black hair framing a small, solemn face. There was no mistaking Emilie.

Or Maggie.

15

Faith usually lunched with friends after church on Sunday, but today she sought the peaceful solitude of her cottage. She warmed up some leftover pasta and ate contentedly with Watson. The week had been full and hectic, not only with retreat obligations but with the fallout from Emilie's death. Saturday's confrontations with Wilhelmina and Maggie had left her mind whirling with questions and her spirit somewhat dented.

She'd kept Brooke in the loop about what was going on, but there hadn't been sufficient time to really talk over the details with her. Faith missed her friend. *Stop the pity party*, she chided herself.

"And what do you think of all this, Watson?" she asked the cat curled in her lap.

Watson stirred reluctantly and resettled himself with a surging purr.

Strange how he had been sitting on that framed faded photograph in Maggie's room. Had the photo fallen to the floor in the chaos of whatever had occurred moments before she and Eileen had arrived? Faith had stared in astonishment at the photograph, certain that she was looking at a young Maggie with an even younger Emilie in a pose of tender regard, which didn't line up with the account Maggie had given of their childhood.

She tried to square that image with Maggie, who crossed her arms over her baggy sweater, declaring with great sarcasm that she had nothing to do with "Miss Emilie." Maggie had severed ties with her family and refused even to accompany Bentley to identify the body of her deceased half sister. *I never wanted nothing from them.* And what was that about Bentley's bidding? Brother and sister against disinherited half sister? But Maggie kept a photo of Emilie at her bedside. It didn't make any sense.

"And why would someone break into her shop?" she asked Watson, knowing he was far off in feline dream territory. "What's with all the break-ins anyway? The Emily Dickinson Suite, my cottage, maybe Devon Hamlin's store, and now Maggie's place. It's like an epidemic."

Was it possible that Wilhelmina had also been in the bait shop looking for the documents? Maggie had seen a thin figure in black running away. Could Wilhelmina have been there after Faith confronted her at the riding stables? With real tears and deep contrition, Wilhelmina had confessed only to breaking into Faith's cottage. Had that all been an act by a clever young woman? But how could she have beaten Faith and Eileen to Maggie's shop?

Was Maggie acting too? Her ruddy face had gone ashen when Faith produced the fishing lure. Was it possible she had been on that cliff with Emilie, finally venting her resentment at being left out of the family estate?

Faith gazed out across the rolling hills beyond the manor, to the bleak sky where a few pale clouds scudded along in a desultory dance. Below, a frenzied ocean rushed to land as though chased by an unseen enemy. Robert Frost's "Once by the Pacific" came to mind. A book of his poems rested on the table beside her and, engulfed in melancholy, she looked it up.

> The shattered water made a misty din.
> Great waves looked over others coming in,
> And thought of doing something to the shore
> That water never did to land before.
> The clouds were low and hairy in the skies,
> Like locks blown forward in the gleam of eyes.
> You could not tell, and yet it looked as if
> The shore was lucky in being backed by cliff,
> The cliff in being backed by continent;

It looked as if a night of dark intent
Was coming, and not only a night, an age.
Someone had better be prepared for rage.
There would be more than ocean-water broken
Before God's last Put out the Light was spoken.

She shivered and closed the book. Maybe she should have gone to lunch with her friends after all, even though Midge, away at a two-day convention, wouldn't have been among them.

Right after returning home from the kennels on Friday, Faith had texted Midge about the tender spot on Carlo's flank, knowing she had already left town. Midge had texted back to say she would see Carlo at Castleton on Monday morning.

Now Faith called her, wanting to hear a friendly voice.

"Any updates on the sweet old Newfie?" Midge asked.

"He's still touchy about it, but he seems fine," Faith replied. "So much has happened while you've been away."

"I leave for a couple of days, and everything falls apart." Midge chuckled, then turned serious. "Are you all right, honey?" She had a discerning intuition, even miles away.

Faith almost groaned but quickly recovered. "I'm fine, but we'll have a good deal to catch up on when you get back. Drive safely. Pick me up on your way to the kennels tomorrow morning."

"Will do. Take care and get some rest. You sound overworked."

After they hung up, Faith closed her eyes. A nap might restore her flagging spirits. After all, that was what Sunday afternoons were for. As a child, she hadn't resented her parents' rule that Sundays be set aside as special. They'd always gone to church in the morning and reserved the afternoon for quiet time, which meant reading or working a puzzle, sometimes watching football with Dad. She had enjoyed cozying up to him on the couch as they shared a bowl of popcorn. Later she'd walk one of the rescue animals Mom invariably sheltered.

When a sudden lump formed in her throat, she realized with surprise that she was homesick. She wouldn't even object to Mom's poorly disguised and inevitable questions about her love life. It was natural, she supposed, to want her daughter suitably settled. Yet this daughter was almost forty and still unattached. *Usually happily so!* She sighed. Death—anyone's death—had a way of making a person feel vulnerable and alone.

A knock on the cottage door brought her sitting bolt upright, dislodging Watson. She wasn't expecting anyone, but perhaps Brooke was stopping by or the tireless Marlene had some errand that couldn't wait. But when she moved the sheer curtain aside, she found Wolfe on the step, with his collar turned up, the wind ruffling his hair.

"I hope I'm not disturbing you," he said when she flung the door open. "If you're busy I can stop by later."

Faith blinked at him, struggling to orient herself. It was never an easy task where Wolfe was concerned. He had a magnetism that always unmoored her. It wasn't just his good looks or his aura of success. It was something less tangible, more bewildering. "Not at all," she managed. "Please, won't you come in?" Why did she sound so stiff?

Wolfe ducked his head slightly and stepped inside. Watson welcomed him by threading himself around his ankles and emitting a raspy meow. Wolfe smiled down at him.

"I was going to make coffee. Can I offer you some?"

"I'd love it. That wind is brutal. It certainly doesn't feel like spring."

"Just push that afghan aside," she said, indicating the sofa near the fireplace and heading into the kitchen. "I'll be right back."

"Are you sure it's no trouble?"

"Of course not." Faith waved off his question, feeling suddenly better. She was glad she'd brought home some of Aunt Eileen's homemade peanut butter cookies after their meeting at Candle House. She placed them on the Wedgwood plate her sister, Jenna, had given her for Christmas.

This was the second time in four days that Wolfe had visited her at the cottage. He had come on Wednesday to express concern that she had been the one to discover Emilie's body. And here he was again. Was there something in her friends' teasing about his being around more often since her arrival?

Snap out of it! Faith placed cups and saucers on her fleur-de-lis tray alongside the coffee and cookies and returned to the living room.

Watson had made himself comfortable on the rumpled afghan near Wolfe's leg. She gently shooed him away, lest his whiskers get too close to the cookies, and poured coffee into two cups. Watson leaped onto the back of the sofa behind Wolfe's head, and she gave up.

Wolfe took a long drink of the steaming brew and released a satisfied sigh. "Best coffee I've had all day. And who can turn down homemade cookies?" He reached for one and smiled, making his blue eyes sparkle. She liked the little laugh lines at their corners, which on a man—well, one man in particular—looked fantastic and on women were known ingloriously as crow's-feet.

Faith sat down across from him. "Aunt Eileen made them, and I claimed some to take home."

"My compliments to Aunt Eileen," Wolfe said, helping himself to another. He was quiet for several seconds and then set his cup down and leaned back against the sofa. His eyes turned serious. "Marlene told me what happened here the other night. She said you thought someone was in your cottage while you were out."

She nodded. She knew Marlene wasn't convinced of the break-in, and she had even accused Faith of imagining things. "Someone *was* in my cottage," she amended. "And I know who it was."

He frowned and waited.

"Wilhelmina Hodge, the youngest of the poetry retreat guests. Her poem was 'Daddy's Visit.'" Faith mentioned the title because Wolfe had attended the poetry reading in which Wilhelmina had participated.

"The poem about the kitten?" Wolfe asked.

"That's the one. She sticks close to Martha Weathers, a retired teacher from New Brunswick."

He said nothing, eyes intent on her face. Absently, he stroked Watson, who had returned to his place on the rumpled afghan.

"Wilhelmina was looking for the documents Emilie bragged about, but she didn't get very far thanks to Watson. He did one of his flying leaps on her head when she snuck in my pantry window and scared her out of her wits. She bolted out the front door without searching the cottage." The humor of it struck Faith now as she told the story. "Besides, the documents weren't here anyway."

"How did you know it was her?" Wolfe asked, a trace of a smile appearing.

"Wilhelmina has a particular odor about her, probably her acne medicine, and I smelled it when I came home that night. Yesterday I confronted her near the riding stables, and she confessed. Apparently, she did it because she wanted to protect Dickinson's name from slanderous gossip." Faith quickly sketched in the story as the young woman had told it to her.

Wolfe shook his head. "Crazy and very sad. It's a good thing you turned those documents over to the police."

"Yes, and Marlene agreed to make sure everyone at the retreat is aware of that."

"She did," Wolfe confirmed, moving to the edge of the sofa and reaching into the inside pocket of his jacket. "But I've gone one better on that score. I had this put in today's paper." He withdrew a small folded section, opened it, and handed it to her.

She quickly read the short article.

Local police continue to investigate the drowning of Miss Emilie Smythe, who at the time of her death was attending a poetry retreat at Castleton Manor in Lighthouse Bay. The management and guests of the retreat have cooperated fully in the matter and have turned over historical documents tied to Amherst poet Emily Dickinson to the authorities. The materials are being examined for authenticity by experts in an undisclosed location.

"That should put to rest any spurious ideas of absconding with potentially valuable artifacts," Wolfe said.

"I'm so sorry," Faith said. "No one wants to see negative press connected with Castleton Manor."

"Nor do we want to jeopardize the safety of our guests and staff," Wolfe said gently. "It's bad enough that you and your friends had to find her."

Faith was touched by the concern in his voice. "I appreciate that. I was glad to get those documents out of my house. I never wanted them in the first place, but Emilie was so insistent. I can't quite understand why she suddenly changed course and gave up the theory that she was related to Dickinson. She was in such distress." She recalled the torment she had read in the woman's dark, soulful eyes. After a moment she added, "It's been hardest on Bentley, I think."

"Yes, well . . ." He cleared his throat. "Speaking of Bentley, he's gone back to the Vineyard because he had some business that couldn't be handled here. He wanted me to let you know." Wolfe dropped his gaze. "He asked me to say goodbye."

Why had Bentley felt it necessary to tell her he was leaving? They'd gone out only once, and as far as she was concerned it was merely to find out information about his sister. Well, mostly. "I see," she said simply. Faith wasn't sure what she read in Wolfe's eyes when he looked up at her. A question? A warning? She reached for the coffeepot. "Would you like a warm-up?" she asked lightly.

"No thanks." Wolfe refolded the newspaper and tucked it back into his jacket. "I should leave you to enjoy your afternoon. I just wanted you to know about this." He tapped the place where he'd put the paper. "And to make sure you're all right."

"Thank you." She felt oddly distressed that he was about to leave. "Have you heard if there have been any breaks in the case? It's all been so upsetting."

"The police have been out a time or two to search the area, but I'm afraid they've been rather secretive about it." He gave her a searching look. "You may know more about it than they do." The laugh lines at the corners of his eyes deepened.

That Faith got involved in mysteries was no secret, and Wolfe hadn't been shy about praising her efforts in the past. She looked away with a slightly embarrassed smile.

"But it could be dangerous to go digging up clues," he said, caution darkening his eyes. "The police will work it out." He paused as though considering whether to say more.

"My aunt and I met Emilie's half sister yesterday," she admitted.

"I'm sure she didn't exactly invite you in for coffee," Wolfe said knowingly. "A crusty old salt, that one."

Faith bit the inside of her lip. "Actually, we needed some bait."

"Fishing?" he asked. "Ice fishing?"

"Aunt Eileen likes hunting for the spring bass. She's a surprising outdoorsman—uh, woman. There wasn't any ice, and we weren't the only ones fishing along the pier."

He shook his head.

But Faith went on. "Did you know someone broke into Maggie's shop too? It was shortly before we arrived. She was pretty livid, but she eventually calmed down." She didn't dare mention the shotgun.

A frown furrowed his forehead. "Did the police say what the intruder was after?"

"Maggie wouldn't call them. She said they've been swarming all over her place and she didn't want them around anymore. Besides, she scared off the would-be thief. Whoever is after those historical documents must know of her connection to the Smythe family, even though she says she has nothing to do with them. I just hope whoever it is will read the papers and stop looking for them."

Wolfe got up, still shaking his head. "I'm worried about you, Faith," he said without a trace of humor. "There's a dark streak in that family—maybe more than one dark streak—and I don't want you to get caught up in their web."

Surprised at the intimacy of his tone, Faith said nothing as she stood. What did Wolfe mean by "a dark streak" and "caught in their web"? He'd been around Cape Cod all his life. What did he know about Emilie's family, especially Bentley? He hadn't warned her directly about him, but everything in his voice and body language spoke of distrust.

"Thanks for the coffee and cookies. It's always good to see you." Wolfe met her eyes. "If you should need anything . . ."

Faith didn't trust herself to speak. There was something so comforting, so tender in his gaze. Had she read something into his look, his tone, that wasn't really there? Something she only hoped was there? She pushed her thoughts aside and smiled at him. "Thank you for the newspaper statement and for watching out for all of us."

And then he was gone, hunching his shoulders as he stepped into the spring wind.

16

Sleep came hard on Sunday night after Wolfe's visit, but Faith was up and ready when Midge's light blue Subaru Forester pulled up the drive to her cottage. She watched her friend emerge, looking far too put together for having just arrived from a two-day convention and driven six hours to get home. Her signature fuchsia lipstick complemented her pink sweater coat and high-fashion boots. Midge had style, even if she was only going on a routine veterinary visit.

Or not so routine. The big Newfie was healing well from the mange, but the matter of the sore spot on his flank still worried Faith.

She opened the door wide to welcome Midge. "You must need coffee. Come on in and set a spell." Midge's Alabama roots often inspired a greens-and-grits greeting.

Midge gave Faith a hug and slipped out of her boots. "Peter made me coffee first thing this morning," she said, tossing her coat over a chair, "but I could really use another cup. So hand over the coffee quick!"

When they were seated at the kitchen table with mugs of French roast in hand, Faith leaned toward her friend. "I'm glad you're back. It's been a little crazy around here."

"What's been going on? Did the investigation wrap up?"

"Hardly. It just gets curiouser and curiouser, as Lewis Carroll would say." Faith sighed, wondering where to begin to catch her friend up with what had been happening. "To start with, when I got home Friday night after having dinner with Bentley Smythe—"

"You went out to dinner with Bentley Smythe?" Midge gaped at her.

"It wasn't a date. Not really." She wouldn't mention the pink tulips and Bentley's attentiveness. "He just wanted someone to go with him to the new seafood restaurant, and I thought it would be a chance to get some information about Emilie."

"Well, I declare, girl. He's even richer than Wolfe and a hunk to boot!"

Faith ignored her comment, waving a hand as if to proclaim it of no consequence. "What I wanted to tell you is that someone snuck into my cottage through the pantry window and tried to steal the documents Emilie gave me. Of course, they weren't here, but Miss Wilhelmina Hodge didn't know that."

"Wilhelmina Hodge? That's who broke into your house?" Midge twirled a lock of honey-colored hair around her ear and wrinkled her nose. "Who's Wilhelmina Hodge?"

"A guest of the retreat. A troubled young woman and a big fan of Emily Dickinson. As it turns out, she was determined to save Dickinson's reputation. She wanted to burn those documents and stifle all speculation," Faith quickly explained. "I'm pretty sure she didn't have anything to do with Emilie's death, though."

"Oh, honey. This is all getting too scary. You'd think the police would have arrested someone by now. Maybe Devon Hamlin or—well, someone!"

"Speaking of scary, Aunt Eileen and I went fishing by way of Maggie Haggedorn's bait shop. She pointed a shotgun at us and ordered us out of the place because she'd just run off a potential robber. But I spotted lures in her shop that were exactly like the one I pulled out of Watson's fur that day on the beach."

Midge's eyes widened. "Did you confront her about it?"

"Yes. Maggie wasn't pleased when I put the lure under her nose and told her where I found it. She doesn't want anything to do with her family and can't stand 'Miss Emilie.' At least that's what she says, but Watson found a photograph of Maggie with little Miss Emilie looking like the best of pals."

"Well, Watson, you clever boy," Midge cooed, rubbing him behind his ears.

The cat had taken up residence by Midge's feet, probably scrounging for crumbs, and now he arched his back in delight.

"He also chased Wilhelmina out of my cottage by diving on top of her head."

"Three cheers for the animal kingdom!" Midge said. "Atticus would probably have shredded her skirt if he'd been here. Seriously, I'm glad those documents are in the hands of the police."

"A fact Marlene announced to the guests at the manor on Saturday," Faith said. "And Wolfe put a notice in the newspaper to confirm for everyone in the area that there's no point in looking for them because they've been turned over to the police. It meant bad press for Castleton, though. You know how he and Marlene wanted to keep all this out of the news, but he gave the pertinent information to the editor anyway. Actually, I just learned about it yesterday when he came by the cottage to show me the paper."

Midge raised both eyebrows and clasped her hands together. "And how is that gorgeous man these days? I'm glad to see he's looking out for you, but that's no surprise."

"Don't start," Faith warned.

"What?" Midge asked innocently. "I wasn't going to say that it's about time Wolfe Jaxon realized the treasure he has in Castleton Manor's librarian. Really, he's been skirting around commitment for far too long, and I know he's smitten with you."

"You're worse than Brooke," Faith said with mock exasperation. She cleared the coffee cups and plopped them resolutely into the sink. "Come on, Doctor. Let's have a look at Carlo. Watson's raring to go. He's become quite a fan of that Newfie."

Ears perked up like furry arrowheads, Watson trotted to the door. Inside Midge's SUV he took his place on Faith's lap, whiskers quivering, and gazed out the window. When the vehicle came to a halt and the door opened, he raced in the direction of the kennels, waiting for no man—or woman!

Laughing, Faith and Midge followed at a more sedate pace.

"I keep thinking about what a protective breed Carlo is. It's so odd that he never tried to intervene when Emilie was in danger," Faith remarked as she and Midge walked to the end of the row of kennels.

"If someone was out on those rocks threatening Emilie, he would have done something if he could." Midge stopped. "Watson looks distracted, and he's coming back this way."

"That's strange. He's always first at Carlo's kennel and never waits for the door to open. Just slithers in under the bars." Faith hurried forward. "Well, that explains it. Carlo's not here. One of the attendants probably took him for a walk."

They ducked into the animal care center at the south end of the row. Annie Jennings, her thick braid slung over her shoulder, stood at the filing cabinet in the cubicle that passed for an office. As she thumbed through manila folders, she rested one booted foot on a stool and hummed a cowboy ballad—something about a lonesome mountain trail.

"Morning, Annie," Midge called, plunking her black bag on the desk. "We came to check on Carlo, but he doesn't seem to be in his kennel. Someone take him walking?"

The pretty aide turned, twisting the bandanna at her neck. A soft spray of freckles bloomed beneath her large hazel eyes. "Nope. Nobody else here to mind the store." She pushed aside the stool and came around to the desk. "He's been gone only a day, and we already miss the sweet old boy."

"What do you mean?" Faith demanded, a sudden catch in her throat.

"I thought you all knew at the manor," Annie replied. "Mr. Smythe had Carlo picked up early Saturday evening. I'd gone home for the day, and one of the other attendants was in charge."

"Bentley Smythe?" Faith asked. "Bentley came and got him?"

"No, the van from Cruden's Animal Hostel came at sunset. They had a signed order from Mr. Smythe." Annie gave Faith a sympathetic look. The kennel attendant loved animals and dedicated her life to caring for them. Not only did she tend to the animals at the manor, but she and her German-born rancher husband raised horses and a good-sized herd of Angora goats.

Faith was aghast that Bentley had arranged for Carlo to be taken to an animal shelter. How could he do that? But it was Bentley's prerogative to do what he wanted with his sister's property, wasn't it? Just because Faith had taken a liking to the dog, it wasn't up to her to decide what happened to him. But a shelter? She found herself unable to articulate her distress. "Where's Cruden's?" she managed to choke out.

"It's way over on the north end of the Cape," Midge said.

Annie flicked the end of her bandanna over her shoulder and looked helplessly at Faith. "I'm sorry."

Faith turned to the door, eager for fresh air. Watson paced, but he allowed Faith to pick him up and carry him to Midge's SUV. Once inside, he perched in the back window, where he continued to watch for signs of his canine friend.

Midge got in and started the motor.

"I never thought . . . ," Faith began. When Wolfe had told her that Bentley had left Castleton Manor to attend to business, he hadn't said anything about the dog, nor had she given him a thought after arranging to meet Midge this morning. "Bentley said he would do something about Carlo," she whispered, "but I can't believe he would send him to a shelter. And without telling anyone." Well, perhaps he had told someone, but he hadn't mentioned it to her.

"He certainly didn't waste any time," Midge said, pursing her lips disagreeably.

"No, he didn't." Indignation filled her, even as her mind registered the fact that she had only told him that she had become quite fond of the dog. It was Bentley's responsibility to arrange for Carlo's care. The dog couldn't stay at Castleton Manor forever now that his mistress was dead. But Faith felt terrible for Carlo, and she couldn't shake the feeling that he held some clue to Emilie's death.

"What do you want to do?" Midge asked, gripping the steering wheel.

"What I don't want to do is leave Carlo in that animal shelter."

"You want to make sure he's all right, don't you?" Midge said knowingly.

Faith nodded, surprised to feel a lump forming in her throat.

"Then let's go. We should be able to make it there in less than an hour."

"You're a sweetheart," she responded, finding it difficult to speak. "But I can go on my own. I don't have to open the library until later this afternoon. Are you sure you can spare the time?"

For answer, Midge pressed the accelerator and headed for the highway.

The kennels at Cruden's Animal Hostel were clinically clean and filled with noisy, forlorn-looking animals. Many of them had been rescued from neglectful or abusive situations, and others had been left at the shelter because their owners could no longer keep them. Entering the building brought back a flood of childhood memories to Faith. Her mother had harbored many shelter animals over the years.

Watson wasn't the least bit happy about being left in the vehicle. After promising to make it up to him later, Faith made a beeline for the facility's reception area, with Midge hurrying to catch up.

"You'll likely have to pay a stiff fee to adopt," Midge warned her. "Dogs can cost hundreds of dollars. Of course, that pays for their shots and neutering or spaying, and the money keeps these important places in business. Are you prepared for that?"

Faith nodded. "If only Bentley had told me what he was planning, I would have helped to find Carlo a home. It even occurred to me that Maggie might take him. When we saw her on Saturday she had just come from burying her own dog. She was in no mood to consider Carlo then but maybe later." She shook her head. *It probably isn't likely, seeing as how she feels about Emilie.*

"And what will you do with Carlo if we take him out?"

"I don't know, but I don't want to leave him here." *Do I dare ask Wolfe if Carlo can stay at Castleton again temporarily?* If he said no, could Faith keep him at the cottage for the time being? Watson would no doubt be in favor.

Midge approached a young male attendant. "We're looking for a large, well-mannered dog that will be at home on a ranch." Stopping just short of prevarication, she managed to get permission to have a look at a black Newfoundland male they had recently received.

Carlo recognized them instantly, judging from the quick rise of his huge head and the thumping of his tail.

After a few moments of head-scratching and puzzled glances, the attendant left them to acquaint themselves with their potential pet. Faith suspected he was probably dancing for joy that someone might actually take the enormous animal, which Bentley had no doubt pressed upon them, bringing his considerable influence to bear.

"The sore spot is on his left flank," Faith whispered as she gently stroked the dog's head and ears. "Annie discovered it when she was brushing him."

As Midge carefully inspected the area, she frowned. "I'd like to examine him at my clinic and do a little testing. I could be wrong, but it looks like it might be a gunshot wound." Her green eyes clouded. "It could have been caused by buckshot or a stun gun."

Faith felt her pulse quicken, and something turned over in her stomach. A stun gun could disable the animal for a while, but then he would be quite normal again. Had that happened to Carlo? Had someone shot him to render him helpless to aid Emilie?

With a sense of sickening dread, she remembered something Bentley had said about Wolfe almost a week earlier when he had sought her out in the library: *Wolfe and I were friends in college. We once went on a safari together.* Maybe a man who hunted wild animals would be acquainted with a stun gun.

She recalled as well what Wolfe had said when she had asked him about his friendship with Bentley: *I was a green freshman and didn't know the first thing about what I was getting into. I realized shooting animals—in the wild or anywhere else—wasn't for me.* And just yesterday he had spoken of a dark streak in the Smythe family. *Maybe more than one dark streak—and I don't want you to get caught in their web.*

Faith looked at Midge as the words played in her mind. "It can't be, can it?"

"What?"

"Bentley would know how to use a stun gun. He's a hunter."

"I thought the police had ruled him out," Midge said, rising and nodding toward the attendant who had shown them to Carlo's cage.

"So did I." Faith's mind reeled with catapulting thoughts. Did Bentley have a reason for dispatching Carlo so quickly? Had the police missed something? Had she missed something? Something that lay beneath the man's charming, handsome facade?

The stunned attendant beamed at them when Faith declared she'd like to adopt the Newfie. "Come on back and we'll do the paperwork. We haven't had a chance to give him a thorough examination yet, but he seems healthy. And he's been gentle as a lamb."

In less than half an hour, Carlo was safely in the back of Midge's SUV, and they were on the way to Castleton Manor with a watchful Watson standing by.

What am I doing, taking on Carlo? And what lay ahead for them all as the investigation into Emilie's death unfolded? Faith clasped her hands tightly in her lap to keep them from trembling and recalled the chilling lines from Frost's poem.

> *It looked as if a night of dark intent*
> *Was coming, and not only a night, an age.*
> *Someone had better be prepared for rage.*

17

When Faith woke later than usual the next morning, she found Watson curled up beside Carlo on an old quilt she had spread out by the fireplace. "Don't get any bright ideas," she said, standing over them in her robe and slippers. "This isn't a permanent arrangement."

Watson scampered to the kitchen, no doubt to await his breakfast.

The dog heaved himself to a sitting position and surveyed her with soulful eyes. He'd woken her up two hours earlier for a walk. Now Carlo appeared to claim her officially with a great sweep of his tongue.

"None of that," she told him playfully.

She would confess that she'd temporarily adopted Carlo, preferably to Wolfe, but of course Marlene would have to be told, and she would not be happy about it. But the news could wait. First, they needed to learn more about the wound in the dog's flank.

When her duties at the library were completed, she loaded Carlo and Watson into her Honda and arrived at Midge's well-lit, modern office somewhat later than she had planned.

"How did it go?" Midge asked as she led them to her examining room. "Did Carlo bark all night and alert the whole manor to his presence?"

"He didn't make a peep—or a woof," Faith joked. "So, our secret's safe for the time being. It was too late to say anything last night. I'll fess up later and hope Wolfe and Marlene are in a good mood."

"They'll likely think you're crazy, paying over $300 for the big brute."

"Probably," Faith agreed. "But I can't help thinking he's a very important piece of this whole puzzle. And I couldn't just leave him there."

"Exam tables were made for dogs the size of Atticus," Midge mused, patting Carlo's huge head and kneeling at his side. "Not for small horses.

But I think he'll stay quiet enough if we're lucky." She pushed aside the heavy fur on Carlo's left flank. "See that small round red mark?"

Faith leaned in close and studied a mark the size of a pea with a reddened area around it. "You say a stun gun could leave such a mark?"

"Those guns usually have two prongs on them that deliver the jolt of electricity and leave a little round dot or burn." Midge gently swabbed the injured area, murmuring soothingly to the dog. "I think we can easily confirm the kind of implement that was used. In any case, we can conclude that someone shocked this dog into conformity. The electricity works on the muscles of the body, rendering an animal unable to attack. Sometimes it takes more than one or two shocks."

"Poor Carlo," Faith said and smoothed the fur around his neck.

Carlo whimpered, bringing Watson back from whatever he had been exploring in the nearby area.

Midge quickly examined the rest of the dog, then reached for a pup-tart from a canister close at hand and held it out for Carlo. "I'm glad whoever disabled him didn't do any permanent damage. I'll give you some salve that you can administer a couple times a day. That should dull any remaining tenderness." She removed her white smock and scrubbed her hands in the sink. "Let's go to my office and have a cup of coffee."

"You said the magic word," Faith responded.

As Faith sipped the steaming coffee, she tried to absorb the fact that someone had not wanted any interference in their unsavory plan. It wasn't likely that disabling Carlo had been a last-minute thought. She doubted that anyone in the area carried around a stun gun or a prod or whatever it was that had left the burn mark. It must have been planned. Bentley? She didn't want to believe it. Just because he had been a hunter and gone on safaris didn't mean he was guilty of this. What did they really know about Devon Hamlin or Maggie Haggedorn or Wilhelmina Hodge? Or it could have been some unknown person.

"We need to alert Chief Garris about this. And also tell him what happened at Maggie's place on Saturday." Faith shook her head. "This whole mess only gets more and more convoluted. I don't know what to think." She looked across at Midge, who was being uncharacteristically quiet with her lips pursed and her forehead wrinkled in thought.

Midge lifted the phone from her desk and punched in a number. After a long moment, she replaced the receiver. "Remember the bracelet I left with Devon?" She raised an eyebrow. "I've been trying to call the shop all day, but there's been no answer. He may have gone home for the afternoon, but I've heard Devon has always run that business like clockwork."

"That is odd," Faith agreed, remembering their earlier visit to Devon's disheveled shop and the black eye he had tried to hide. "Do you suppose he's in trouble?"

"Or decided to take an unannounced vacation," Midge offered with considerable irony. "Do you want to run over there and look? We can leave Carlo and Watson at the bakery with Sarah. They can have the run of the back room 'til we return."

"If you think she won't mind."

Midge pushed her coffee cup aside and grabbed her sweater coat. "She won't mind, and it won't take us long."

They dropped the animals off and drove to the antique shop in Faith's Honda. Lighthouse Bay exhibited the usual small-town activity, heightened by teasing southerly breezes that hinted at warmer weather to come. Faith loved seeing the towering lighthouse and the multitude of boats in the harbor. But as she recalled the note with its subtle, inscrutable threat, a pall seemed to settle over the familiar scene. It was likely that Emilie had been strangely summoned to this very lighthouse. By whom? And why?

When Faith turned the corner onto the street where Hamlin's Antiques was located, she noticed a small crowd gathered at the far end of the street. "Maybe there's a sale going on—" But she stopped in midsentence when she spotted a patrol car parked along the curb and recognized Chief Andy Garris and Officer Laddy outside Devon's shop.

Midge turned to Faith. "Uh-oh."

They got out of the vehicle and headed to the shop on foot. About half a block from the store, they passed a battered pickup idling at the curb. Inside, a slender man in sunglasses and a black baseball cap was hunched forward in his seat. The truck suddenly lurched away from the curb, coming close to hitting them.

"Watch out!" Midge yelled, yanking Faith out of the way. "He wasn't even looking!"

The truck sped off.

Faith let out an indignant but relieved sigh. At the same time, she was aware of having seen the driver somewhere before. But she shook off the sensation and proceeded to the store with Midge.

Officer Laddy was talking to an elderly couple a few feet from the front door of Hamlin's Antiques.

"The store's been locked up since yesterday," the older gentleman said.

"Any idea where the owner is?" Laddy asked.

Both shook their heads and walked on.

Faith went directly to Chief Garris. "Is something wrong?"

"You two have business with Mr. Hamlin?" he asked without preamble and with a look of serious intent.

"He's repairing a bracelet for me," Midge said. "I couldn't reach anyone on the phone to see if it was done, so Faith and I just came over. What's happened?"

"We have an arrest warrant for Mr. Hamlin. We know he wrote the letter to Miss Smythe about the lighthouse as well as the note passed under Mrs. Weathers's door at Castleton Manor. His prints were on that one. He must have been hoping to deflect suspicion from himself." Garris directed Faith and Midge away from the group of onlookers. "Hamlin had means and opportunity, but confirming the source of the letters is the clincher."

"Chief, we need to talk to you," Faith said.

"Not now. Can you come down to the station?" Without waiting for an answer, he issued an order to Officer Laddy. "Get some men in here and do a thorough search of the premises." With that he climbed into his car, speaking into his cell phone.

"We'll be there right away," Faith called after him and grabbed Midge's hand, which was as cold and unsteady as hers. Wordlessly, they followed the chief's car.

When the reception officer admitted them, Faith and Midge approached the chief at his desk.

He looked up from his active computer screen and gave Faith a welcoming nod.

She had a special relationship with the man so like her own father, but she never exploited it. "Sorry to bother you."

"Sit down. Sit down," he urged with a kind inflection in his voice. "It was you, after all, who put us on to Mr. Hamlin, but unfortunately he's gotten away from us. Until we catch him—and we will—you two need to be cautious. We'll alert the management at Castleton Manor too, but Hamlin's not likely to be anywhere near Lighthouse Bay."

Faith told him about their earlier visit to Devon's shop, the vandalism that seemed apparent and the fact that he looked as though he'd been in a fight.

The chief took some notes as he listened, nodding from time to time. "I'm not sure what all this means. It's definitely strange. But we have documented proof that the note telling Miss Smythe to meet at the lighthouse came from Hamlin's Royal typewriter. We've also confirmed his fingerprints on the bogus suicide note torn from the victim's notebook."

Midge briefly outlined what she had discovered—evidence that a stun gun had been used on Carlo—and Faith described what had transpired at Maggie Haggedorn's bait shop. She did not mention Wilhelmina and the break-in at the cottage nor any of her latest suspicions regarding Bentley, which didn't seem important considering recent events.

Devon Hamlin was guilty after all. Though he had managed to appear nonchalant and protested his innocence where Emilie was concerned, he'd been there on that cliff. The police were on it. Faith had every confidence they would find the man. The truth would come out, and then they could all relax. Despite many unanswered questions, a great wave of relief swept over her.

Midge said little on the short trip back to Happy Tails where they had left Carlo and Watson.

And for Faith, absorbing what the chief had told them overrode any desire to chat. There was an awful lot to be explained, but things were not likely to make sense until Devon had been found and the police could get a confession. It was growing late, and she was eager to get home to her snug cottage and leave the crime solving to the authorities.

"Surely you're not serious!" Marlene exclaimed, gaping at Faith. The assistant manager of Castleton Manor sat at her broad desk, gripping a sheaf of papers, a long stream of tape spiraling from an adding machine at her side. A few strands of hair had escaped her usually tidy bun and strayed over the shoulders of her shantung suit jacket. Something she had been toiling over obviously wasn't coming out to her satisfaction.

Faith realized she'd chosen an inopportune moment to speak to Marlene. After talking to Chief Garris, Faith had walked Carlo, fed him and Watson, and lit a fire with relish as a chill wind had blown through. She had left the cat and dog ensconced on the hearth and returned to the manor to own up to the huge animal lodged at her cottage. Not that he had been a bit of trouble—middle-of-the-night request to go out aside. She'd been unable to locate Wolfe, so here she stood in Marlene's office.

Timing is everything, Faith thought, *and here goes nothing.* "It's only temporary, I assure you," she said with an assurance she didn't feel. "I just couldn't think of that sweet Newfie consigned to an animal shelter."

"It was the wish of his new owner," Marlene said huffily. "Now that Miss Smythe . . ." Her voice dropped, then regained its clarity. "I told Mr. Smythe before he left that he'd have to handle the situation promptly, and he did. I can't believe you turned right around and—what did you do? Adopt him? You know we can't handle an animal of that size in the long term!" Her face turned red.

Faith had the urge to remind her about her blood pressure. But she stopped herself just in time. "There was a very good reason." She schooled herself to be patient. "You see, we had all been wondering why Carlo didn't defend Emilie when she was assaulted. Midge discovered that the dog had been disabled by a stun gun, which the perpetrator must have used. So we knew that Carlo held a clue to what happened."

"And you were doing your Agatha Christie thing again. You simply can't leave matters to the police." Marlene sighed. "Honestly, you were hired to be the librarian here, not super sleuth of the year."

Faith ignored this interruption. "The police are going to arrest Devon Hamlin. Apparently, he's taken off—just left his shop and absconded. But they know he arranged to meet Emilie and that he put that fake suicide note under Martha Weathers's door. He wanted everyone to think Emilie had killed herself. And of course, he was spotted near the scene that day."

A look of amazement sprang to Marlene's features. "Oh! Do they think we're safe here?"

"I'm sure they'll have him in custody soon. As for Carlo, I promise to find him a good home. I think Annie might be happy to have him out at her ranch. She's already taken a liking to him."

Marlene shook her head, gazing down at whatever puzzle she was trying to solve on her desk. After a long moment, she said, "Wouldn't you know Wolfe would decide he had an urgent errand right when I need his help with these ledgers."

Faith waited for her bluster to end. She, too, was sorry to have missed Wolfe. She really wanted to talk to him about everything. She needed his clear head, his understanding.

Marlene looked up, green eyes intense. "I'm sorry I don't have time to chat." The brusque sarcasm had returned, and Faith knew she had royally upset her highness.

"Thanks for understanding," Faith said, backing toward the door. "I'll get out of your hair now."

She left Castleton Manor to walk back to her cottage, feeling the cool rush of wind on her face. Savoring the freshness of the air and the early moonlight gilding bushes and topiaries, she slowed her steps. A few lines of Emily Dickinson's famous poem about the moon whispered on the wind.

> *Her Bonnet is the Firmament—*
> *The Universe—Her shoe—*
> *The Stars—the Trinkets at Her Belt—*
> *Her Dimities—of Blue—*

The moon as a grand lady. Whatever the documents under scrutiny showed, Faith had a sense that Emily Dickinson herself would always be venerated as a grand lady. She could almost understand Wilhelmina's fierce desire to safeguard the poet's reputation. But in the last analysis, all the darkness of man couldn't put out the true light.

Somewhere an owl hooted mournfully. She felt a little shiver and quickened her steps. For all the brightness of the moon, her current path lay in blackness. She would be glad for the refuge of her cottage. Was that a stirring in the bushes? A shadow she hadn't seen before?

Faith decided she was paranoid and hurried forward, humming a tuneless melody she couldn't have named.

The cat watched the slow thump of the dog's tail on the quilt by the fireplace. It had the most amusing rhythm. With a playful swipe, he pushed it down, only to watch it flip up again. It was rather fun, having the huge creature around. There was a limit, though. If the canine stuck his nose in the cat's dish one more time, he'd have to show him who was boss in no uncertain terms.

As though he'd somehow known he was under scrutiny, the dog lifted his head and shook it. He sat up on his haunches to peer down at him. The cat gave him his most superior look and deliberately slapped his tail again. The dog pretended to lunge at him and whined to show he was only playing. Lucky for him!

The cat padded away from the hearth and snooped around. Sometimes the most delightful things could be found under the furniture. Not that his human wasn't a tidy housekeeper, but she'd been too busy lately to remove all the enticing tidbits. His paw touched something under the sofa near the fireplace. The object had a lovely long strip of cloth attached to it. He pulled it out easily with his claw and examined it. Such tantalizing little round balls on it.

He batted it toward the dog, who bravely took on the challenge. He whipped it away in his mouth, tossed it into the air, and grabbed it again in his big white teeth. Soon the two were engaged in a rambunctious game of tug-of-war.

18

Faith turned the key in her cottage door and rushed in with a wave of relief. What was as welcoming as the scent of one's own home? Every house had a unique aroma. Her mother's had always smelled of cinnamon—a spice she favored above all others and used generously—and Grandma's had exuded a mix of lavender and lemon. Her own? Well, she couldn't name it, only that it radiated a scent she knew by no other name than *home*.

A mild thump sounded from the living room followed by the unmistakable scuffling of two pets she had left snoozing by the fire. She dropped her coat on the chair in the hall and went to investigate.

Carlo was in the process of flipping something in the air over his head, with Watson crouched to pounce on it when it landed.

"What are you two doing?" After a moment, it became clear that they were tussling with the Victorian reticule Emilie had given her and which she had carelessly tossed onto the floor a few days earlier. It must have wedged between the sofa and the fireplace or been kicked under the sofa.

The two animals froze. Carlo slunk down, his head on his paws. Watson hopped onto the sofa with what could only be described as a smug grin that said in no uncertain terms, "It wasn't me."

"Look what you've done," Faith scolded, but she wasn't too upset. The ungainly bag with all its gaudy beading was far from inspiring, though she had admired it to stimulate conversation with Emilie. Now she picked it up, limp and slathered in saliva. The strap was torn almost completely off, and the fabric was ripped in several places.

"That's what I get for leaving you two untended." What had she been thinking? At least it wasn't one of her good shoes or the furniture, which Watson had never threatened before. But a large dog confined in small quarters had to have something to do. She shook her head at him, trying hard not to smile because he looked so guilty and forlorn.

With a sigh, Faith went to the kitchen. She returned with a towel to wipe the bag dry enough to explore the damage. The strap and the missing beads—assuming she could find them—could be sewed back on easily enough, but the lining would have to be patched and repaired by a seamstress cleverer than she. *I don't know what I'll do with the thing anyway,* she mused.

Examining it more closely, she discovered that there was more than one layer lining the bag. She separated the coarse burlap-like stuff from the smoother material, and to her astonishment something fell into her hand.

It was green and glass-like and translucent, carved in the shape of a graceful bird. Her breath caught in her throat. She had never seen anything so lovely. How had it been hidden all this time in its ugly shell? She turned it over and over, felt the cool, satiny finish, and held it up to the lamplight. It glowed with emerald brilliance. Could this be real jade? Maybe even real Chinese jade, which could sell for more money than gold? She had seen only pictures and replicas.

What was Emilie doing with a jade figurine concealed in the Victorian bag she'd worn across her chest? Was this what Devon Hamlin had been after? Not the historical letters? A great shiver pulsed through her. The beautiful bird trembled in her hands, and the astonished gasp echoing in the living room was her own.

A knock on the door paralyzed her. She wasn't expecting anyone. The jade bird felt suddenly hot. It burned her hand like a green coal. She quickly pressed it beneath a fringed sofa pillow and stared at the door.

"Faith, it's Brooke! Are you home?"

The familiar voice broke through her fear, and Faith hurried to open the door.

"You are home." Brooke frowned at her. "Are you all right? You look like you've seen a ghost."

"Come in," she croaked. She caught her friend's arm and drew her into the living room. "I haven't seen a ghost, but I've seen something that takes my breath away."

"You're scaring me. What is it? And what's that?" She pointed at Carlo, still moping on the quilt by the fireplace. "What's Emilie's dog doing here?"

Faith sighed and sank down on the sofa. "I'll tell you all about it, but first, sit down. Let me catch my breath." She put both hands to her temples, then jumped up again. She locked the door and closed the blinds and curtains.

Brooke stared at Faith, her eyes as big as harvest moons. "I heard Marlene say the police were looking for Devon Hamlin. I can't believe I actually dated the guy. Diva and Bling were right about him all along. You haven't seen him, have you? He hasn't—"

"No. The chief doesn't think he's anywhere nearby, and they have an all-points bulletin out for him. But I found this." She reached under the sofa pillow and removed the jade bird. She held it in her palm for Brooke to see.

"Oh!" Brooke gently touched it with a finger. "It's exquisite. It looks like jade—and not just any jade. I bet this is the very finest grade." Her eyes flashed with excitement. "You know how I love jewelry, and I was reading about this year's Shanghai World Jewelry Expo. Auctioneers put the opening bid for high-grade jade items at more than a hundred dollars a gram. That's three or four times the price of gold. Jade has even proven to be a better investment than real estate. Where on earth did you find it?"

Faith gestured to the ruined bag on the floor. "Carlo and Watson were playing tug-of-war with it. I left the house for only a few minutes to talk to Marlene, and when I came back the antique bag was pretty well mangled. The figurine fell out as I was trying to put the pieces back together."

Brooke took the bird from Faith's hand and cradled it almost reverently. "What do you suppose Emilie was doing with it?"

"That's the question, isn't it? All this time, we thought someone was after the historical materials. The jade bird must be what Devon wanted all along," Faith said, gazing at the figurine in Brooke's hand. "Remember that note telling Emilie to meet him at the lighthouse? The police have confirmed that it was typed on Devon's old Royal typewriter. Not very smart of him to use such a distinctive method to set up a meeting."

Brooke frowned. "Believe me, Devon is a clever collector and jeweler, but he can be impulsive when it comes to something he wants."

"But he didn't get the figurine because Emilie had hidden it." So why was Devon attacked and his shop ransacked? Was someone else searching for the treasure and thought Devon had gotten it?

"Why was Emilie carrying around this bird figurine?" Brooke mused. "I wonder if it was some kind of symbol for her."

"Maybe it made her think of Dickinson's poem about hope. You know the one." Faith recited:

'Hope' is the thing with feathers—
That perches in the soul—
And sings the tune without the words—
And never stops—at all.

"And poor Emilie paid the price for not turning it over," Brooke said sadly. "But what do you think she was doing with it? Where did she get it?" She put the jade bird back in Faith's hands with trembling fingers. "Your cottage was broken into too. All this time you've been in danger!"

"Yes, but I don't believe the break-in here had anything to do with the figurine. Wilhelmina Hodge admitted climbing in through my pantry window, but she did it because she wanted to end the speculation about her favorite poet. Remember I told you how her father experienced tragedy because of unfounded gossip. Wilhelmina really was after the documents. At least that's what I thought after talking with her but . . ." Faith shook her head. "My mind is still spinning with questions."

"You have to go to the police with this."

"Absolutely."

"I mean now. You can't have this valuable thing in your house or in your possession a minute longer." Brooke rose from the couch and paused to stroke Watson, who had been watching from the top edge of the sofa, eyes bright and alert. Carlo lifted his head from the quilt and whined softly. "I guess we have these two to thank for adding to the mystery. Why isn't Carlo at the kennels?"

"I learned that Bentley had arranged for a shelter to pick him up. Midge and I went there and adopted him. Well, temporarily. I couldn't leave him. Besides, I was sure that sore spot on his flank held a clue to what happened to Emilie. Midge says it was caused by a stun gun. I think whoever killed Emilie stunned Carlo first so he couldn't protect her."

Brooke's eyes clouded. "That's awful. But you've got to do something about *that*." She pointed to the jade bird still clutched in Faith's hand. "We need to take it to the police immediately. We can drop Carlo off at the kennels on the way. Watson will be all right here unless you want to let him come along." She was all business now, walking briskly toward the door. "Where's your coat? Wrap that thing up, and let's get it out of here!"

Faith knew Brooke was right, and she was grateful for the presence of her friend. She went to the kitchen, pulled a paper sack from the drawer, and wrapped the bird in it. She set the bag inside her old tapestry tote and slipped into the coat Brooke was holding out for her. "Leave your car here. We'll take mine. You won't want Carlo to shed on your good upholstery."

Before leaving him with one of the kennel workers, Faith fondled Carlo's ears. "I'll be back for you," she told him. "After all, if it wasn't for you—and your comrade in arms—we might never have found this." She patted the tote at her side.

Carlo gave her a trusting doggy grin.

She picked up Watson, and they were off to unload their dangerous treasure.

"I can't get over it," Brooke said as they motored onto the road leading toward Lighthouse Bay's town center. "Just this week I was researching jade on the Internet. There's a big exposé out now about Burmese jade barons reaping high profits while the laborers live in derelict conditions in the jade fields. It's almost like the gold rush of the 1800s. Jade seekers go in search of high-quality stone and become virtual puppets in the hands of the black marketers. Drugs are rampant in the camps too."

"I think I read something about that," Faith said thoughtfully. She was fascinated by what she was hearing, but at the same time, she felt her nerves jumping, especially when headlights appeared in her rearview mirror. The current stretch of road seemed darker, more desolate than Faith remembered. She'd be glad when they could see the lights of the town.

"Jadeite is preferable to nephrite and commands a higher price because it comes in more vivid greens and other colors and has a finer translucence," Brooke explained. "The demand from wealthy Chinese buyers is driving its value through the roof."

"You're a veritable fountain of information. I hope the police can figure out what all this has to do—" Faith stopped because the headlights behind her were nearly blinding. "Why can't people drive the speed limit and not try to get ahead of everyone else?"

Brooke whirled around just as the vehicle behind slammed into Faith's Honda.

The jolt sent Watson flying off the headrest where he had been snoozing.

Faith felt her head whip forward and back. With a sinking feeling, she realized that this was no accident. The lights blinded her to whoever was behind the wheel, but he intended to stop them. She knew they were in trouble.

Big trouble.

"He's trying to force us off the road!" Brooke screamed.

Faith gripped the wheel, her heart hammering in her chest. She pressed the accelerator, but the determined vehicle kept coming—closer and closer. Suddenly, it swerved around her, causing her to veer sharply to the left and onto a narrow road, then fell in behind her again. *Dear God, help!* she cried silently.

"Your phone, Faith!" Brooke shouted. "I left mine at work. Stupid!" She reached for Faith's tapestry bag, but her hand was jerked away by another jolt from the rear.

Faith glanced in the rearview mirror, and her heart lurched in terror when she made out a pickup. It was the same pickup that had nearly knocked over her and Midge when they walked toward Devon's shop. She had intuited something familiar about the man driving, but in the confusion over Devon's disappearance and the police breaking into the shop, she hadn't considered him further. Now with sudden clarity she recalled the man in the black nylon jacket who had talked to Bentley the night of the poetry reading.

But there was no more time to think. They were struck once more and then sideswiped. Faith was helpless to keep from careening onto the sloping shoulder and down into the ditch beside it. The Honda came to a halt.

"Get out!" a voice commanded.

Faith heard it as though from far away. She was aware that her SUV had remained upright and that she was in one piece as far as her trembling body could surmise. "Brooke, are you okay?"

Beside her, Brooke climbed off the floor and onto the seat. "I'm all right."

"Out. Now!" came the voice, low and hard and completely unfamiliar.

The door to the Honda was yanked open, and Faith saw the glitter of steel. A man in dark clothes with curly black hair beneath a baseball cap stood there. His features were obscured by a pair of huge sunglasses. How did he see in the dark?

The man waved a gun in their faces. "Don't try anything stupid if you know what's good for you."

Half-dazed, Faith stumbled out with Brooke following. Where was the tapestry bag? It must have fallen off the seat when he rammed her bumper. If only she'd kept her cell phone in her pocket, but it was in the bag along with the jade figurine.

The man peered around them into Faith's vehicle. "I'll just make sure you haven't left anything important behind." With a satisfied smirk, he snatched the tapestry bag from the floorboard along with the keys still dangling from the ignition. "Empty your pockets. Hurry up or I'll do it for you."

Faith and Brooke turned their pockets inside out, small change, tissues, and assorted trinkets dropping onto the ground.

"Now get into the truck!" he shouted.

They climbed in, Faith first and then Brooke, both into the only seat in the cab. They'd practically be on top of one another.

"Watson!" Faith called.

The cat leaped up to get in the truck beside her.

But the man roughly shoved him away. "We're not taking that mangy animal," he snarled. "Scram!"

The cat yowled as the nasty human's shoe connected with his flank. The door slammed shut as he tried once more to jump into the truck.

He had to go with his person. She needed him now more than ever. He wouldn't let this evil human separate them.

As the truck lurched and sped forward, the cat let loose a strangled cry of panic. Marshaling all his feline strength, he raced after the fleeing monster. Then he gave a mighty leap—higher and faster than he had ever leaped before.

"Please. We can't leave him here." But Faith's pleas fell on deaf ears, and she watched in anguish as the man ran around to the driver's side, hopped into the seat, and stomped on the accelerator.

She peered over her shoulder, hoping to catch a glimpse of Watson, and as they lurched away, she spotted her beloved pet soaring into the bed of the truck. Faith nearly exploded with joy but stopped herself just in time. The man hadn't seen it. *Now if Watson will only keep his head down.*

"Where are you taking us?" she demanded.

He gave no answer or even a hint that he had heard, though she was near enough that she had to strain toward Brooke to keep her shoulder from bumping against his. He smelled like garlic and stale sweat. Shuddering, she tried to see his face in her peripheral vision. The messy black hair and goggle-like sunglasses had altered his appearance, but it was the same man. He had appeared trim and well-groomed as he stood with Bentley in the library.

The truck swerved again, this time onto a barren road that seemed a million miles from town. Miles from civilization and help. They bumped over the rutted road, their bodies jostling against one another. Faith prayed that Watson was all right in the back, that he had dug his claws into something that would keep him from flying out. Beside her, Brooke shivered.

After several more minutes of bumping and rolling and grim silence from their captor, Faith made out a cobbled driveway that wound down into a wooded hollow, and in a few seconds the shape of a surprisingly large cabin appeared in the truck's headlights. It was hedged with shadowy evergreens and foreboding bushes.

Faith glanced sideways at the man transporting them to whatever doom lay ahead. He leaned slightly forward as he plunged the truck down farther, then veered around the cabin to a wooded area and stopped. The gun reappeared in his left hand. He waved it silently, inclining his head to the passenger door.

Faith and Brooke exited the truck and were prodded ahead. Faith dared not look back to see if Watson was still there.

"Walk," he commanded.

He led them to the cabin, pushed open the door, and motioned them through a rough-hewn foyer and into a spacious, firelit room with tastefully rustic furniture and golden log walls. Every wall was mounted with animal heads, among them a startled-looking stag with a huge rack of antlers and a ferocious gray wolf that might leap into the room and devour them. Faith was aware of others—a leopard with terrifying fangs, a red fox.

A creaking sound tore her attention from the animal trophies to a swivel rocker poised near the fireplace.

From its leather confines a figure slowly emerged. Bentley Smythe stood before them, a smile on his handsome face. "Ladies, I've been waiting for you. Do come in and sit down by the fire. I'm sure you're chilled and would like some refreshment."

19

Faith felt her mouth fall open, heard her heart beat loud enough to be audible. Bentley? Had he been behind all this from the beginning? Had he kidnapped them, had them brought here? It was almost more than she could take in, but as she stared at the man she had tried to comfort and befriend, things began to sift and fall into place in her mind.

I used to own a hunting cabin not far from here, he had said when she'd first met him. He had claimed Wolfe was an old buddy from college who had gone with him on safari. The trophies of his wild game hunting were displayed all around the cabin he obviously still owned. Did anyone else know about this place concealed in the woods?

The man who had run them off the road and dragged them here stood obediently by the door, holding Faith's tapestry bag. If he were groomed and dressed in well-tailored clothes, he might pass for Bentley's brother.

"Thank you, Gregory," Bentley said, looking over their heads to address the swarthy man. "You run along and take care of Miss Newberry's vehicle while I entertain the ladies." His voice was suave, sophisticated, chilling.

The meaning was clear. Gregory's mission was to hide any evidence that she and Brooke had ever been on that desolate road. And Faith had little doubt that Bentley's idea of entertainment would have dire consequences for them.

Gregory handed the tapestry bag to Bentley before he left.

Bentley turned to Faith, his smile fixed and smug. "Well, you certainly took your time returning my property. I've been searching for it, you know." He cocked his head as though slightly amused. "You've caused me no end of trouble. Fortunately, my man was watching tonight when you made your little discovery. It only became necessary to invite you here after you'd parted from that animal you apparently admire so much."

So, she hadn't been paranoid when she thought she saw a shadow moving about the Castleton grounds as she walked home after her visit with Marlene. The ignoble Gregory had been there, as he had been on Devon Hamlin's street and who knew where else, watching her, waiting for his moment.

Faith steeled herself for whatever might be coming, but before it did, there were things she wanted to know. Her fear began to dissolve in a flood of anger. "Are you afraid of Emilie's dog because you shot him and he's likely to remember you?"

"Vicious animals have to be subdued," he said with a note of surprise. "Man rules over the animal kingdom. That's the natural order of things."

"And is it the order of things to betray your own family?"

Bentley drew a long breath, but he didn't lose the placating smile. "Come now. I've hardly betrayed my family. Emilie turned on me. All these years I've protected her, ensured she was comfortable. And all I asked in return was that she make a few special deliveries for me in the course of her travels."

"Deliveries? Like illegal jade, perhaps?" Faith forced herself to keep her gaze on his face rather than on the tapestry bag in his hands, knowing he was eager to rip it open and grasp his prize. Her mind was turning over Emilie's strange words: *I can't do this anymore.* What if she had been referring to making those so-called special deliveries? Doing Bentley's bidding, as Maggie had put it. And what if, when confronted on that lonely cliff, Emilie had refused to continue? Instead, she had given the antique bag with its treasure to Castleton Manor's librarian. "Emilie refused to be your mule any longer, and you killed her."

Bentley's face gradually drained of color, and the veins in his temples throbbed. "No!" A sudden strangled response. "I didn't want to hurt her! She wouldn't listen to reason. But I had to get her to give it to me." He shook his head as though to erase some terrible scene. "She was supposed to hand it over to Devon, but she betrayed him too. She never showed up at the lighthouse like he told her to."

The contents of the threatening note whisked through Faith's mind.

The lighthouse at ten.
Prithee don't fail me.
The saints are watching—
anon they hail thee.

The writer was clearly trying to intimidate Emilie, though she must have known that what she was doing for her brother wasn't right.

"What have you done with Devon?" Brooke, who hadn't spoken until now, demanded. Her eyes flashed in the firelight. "Where is he?"

But it was as if Bentley hadn't heard. "I believed Devon was holding out on me." He bit his lip and turned his gaze away from them. "But Emilie didn't carry out my orders. I thought I could get her to listen, but she wouldn't. Then she tripped. I tried to stop her. She hit her head, and she didn't get up."

"And you left her there," Faith accused.

"Stop it!" Bentley wailed. "Stop it!" He was totally changed, no longer the suave businessman, the entrepreneur who knew what to say in every situation.

Faith imagined him with gloved hands around his sister's arms, driven by greed, angrily shaking her. Perhaps he hadn't meant to kill her, but he had certainly planned his confrontation, down to making sure Carlo couldn't come to the rescue. But how had he gotten the authorities to believe his alibi?

"What are you going to do with us?" Faith hated the shudder in her voice.

Bentley didn't respond but dropped his head into his hands. The tapestry bag dangled between his knees as he bent forward in the chair, his arms folded around himself. "She wouldn't listen! I didn't mean to!" He began to rock like a hurt child seeking comfort.

Faith grabbed Brooke's hand. Was it possible they could run? Bentley was sure to have a gun, though she hadn't seen it yet. And he would know how to use it, to which the animal heads staring down at them could attest. But there would be no chance at all once the despicable Gregory returned. And Bentley was now in some altered state of remorse. She gave Brooke an urgent look, tugging at her hand, and together they sprang for the door.

They fled into the night, not knowing where they were going, but the thick cover of trees that had seemed so menacing now sheltered them in tangled arms. In and out of clusters of bushes and trees they ran, even when they heard footsteps behind them.

"Come back!" The voice was still un-Bentley-like. "You don't need to run," he cajoled. "Come back and have some refreshment. I won't hurt you."

Faith had zero confidence of that. "Come on," she whispered to Brooke. But where were they running—toward the road or back to the cabin?

When they heard a car approach, they froze behind a hedge of prickly yew bushes intertwined with vines and weeds, then peered into the distance. Was Gregory coming back? With pounding hearts, they waited.

"Oh, Miss Newberry!" A childlike call, as though they were playing hide-and-seek, rang out nearby. "I know you're there. Come out, come out, wherever you are!"

Faith flinched.

The footsteps hesitated and seemed to change direction.

They crouched low, hearing a soft rustling of bushes very close by. Faith clutched Brooke's hand. She didn't dare speak—even in a whisper. The rustling continued. It was soft, slow, and steady. Not like human steps. Was it some night animal? Had they unwittingly trespassed in its den?

Suddenly a low meow penetrated her fear. Watson jumped across a fallen branch and into Faith's lap.

"Watson!" she whispered joyously. "You've found us, you brave boy!" She hugged him tight, stroking the cold fur and whispering for him to be quiet.

They waited for what seemed an eternity. Then a light flashed through the trees and with it, the sounds of crashing footsteps and the crunch and whine of wheels.

Before she could stop him, Watson slipped away from Faith and darted into the underbrush.

"Watson!" she hissed.

"Who do you think is out there?" Brooke asked, peeking through the chaos of branches and evergreen scrub.

"I don't know, but I sure hope they're on our side." Faith couldn't suppress the surge of hope and prayed that help was really on the way.

Bentley wasn't calling anymore, but she heard other voices in the distance. The words were undecipherable. The light of a powerful flashlight flashed nearer, almost blinding her as she tried to see who was out there. Branches broke as someone came crashing through the trees.

Crouched in the bracken, Faith felt her heart thudding in her chest, and she squeezed her eyes shut. Bentley knew these woods intimately. He would find them and—

"Faith!"

The voice wasn't Bentley's, and it was blessedly familiar. As were the strong arms going around her and the unique, virile fragrance that embraced her.

A wave of relief swept over her as a face appeared, illuminated by a flashlight. "Wolfe!"

Watson meowed at her feet.

"He led me right to you. Come on, you two. Let's get you out of here." With an arm around each of them, Wolfe shepherded Faith and Brooke past the cabin and into the car, which was still running and thankfully warm.

Watson purred his approval as Faith cuddled him close and whispered praise for bringing Wolfe to them.

The whine of sirens descended on the quiet woods. Lighthouse Bay's finest were swarming the place.

Out of the corner of her eye, she saw a bewildered Bentley being led away to a waiting police car.

Aunt Eileen stepped inside Castleton's library and immediately threw her arms around Faith. "Thank goodness! I couldn't get here fast enough when Marlene phoned. Are you all right, honey?" She searched her niece's face, her own etched in concern. "And, Brooke, are you okay?" she added, reaching out to draw her in too.

Faith, Brooke, and Wolfe had entered the manor a short while ago and retreated to the library with its welcoming ambience that Faith had come to love, to regard as home. Someone had lit a fire. It glowed on the elegant tapestries and floor-to-ceiling shelves of books and highlighted the crimson furniture and carpets.

"Marlene phoned me as soon as Wolfe warned her that you and Brooke were in trouble," Eileen said as she ushered them to the grouping of couches and chairs by the fire.

"But how did you . . . ?" Faith began but let the question trail off as Marlene and Chief Garris approached the gathered group. He had left Bryan Laddy and the other officers to handle the arrest. Faith shivered as she recalled the anguished and surprised look on Bentley's face when he was led away.

Wolfe seated Faith next to him on one of the small couches, his shoulder close to her own.

"H-how did you know? How did you find us?" Faith stammered. Was it her imagination, or did Wolfe press closer to her as though to assure her of his comforting presence? She met his eyes, those marvelous eyes like a clear sky shining through glass.

"I've been looking into the activities of my old college friend." Wolfe shook his head slowly. "Bentley was involved in some shady deals in the past, but for a long time his record seemed clean. But talking to some of his current business partners was enlightening. I also learned that his name is still on the deed for that cabin he said he'd sold long ago."

"I've never seen a place so . . . desolate," Faith said with an unbidden shudder. "It's a wonder anyone knew it existed."

Wolfe swept a hand across his jaw. "When Marlene told me what Midge discovered about Carlo, I went to your cottage right away, but you were gone."

"We were both worried that something was wrong," Marlene broke in. "Especially when Brooke didn't come right back and report to me tonight like she said she would." The assistant manager's hair was uncharacteristically mussed, and shadows darkened her face.

Watson, who had padded off to explore his familiar haunts, now returned and curled up on Faith's lap, as though to ensure he wouldn't be abandoned again.

At the sight of him, Marlene pushed back a little in her chair but gave an obliging shrug in Faith's direction. Perhaps in her worry, she could forgive Watson for being a cat.

"We were on our way to take the jade to the police station when Bentley's sidekick ran us off the road and forced us into his truck," Brooke told them.

"We've had our eye on Mr. Smythe," Chief Garris cut in. "And Gregory Gnome, who by the way was the one who boarded the flight that gave Smythe his alibi. They look enough alike that they could pull it off. But we found proof that Smythe was in town the day his sister died. He'd paid for two flights and taken the earlier one."

"How did you find out about the jade?" Faith asked.

The chief folded his arms across his broad chest. "When we picked up Devon Hamlin, he told us. He was Miss Smythe's contact here at Lighthouse Bay, but she apparently refused to continue being her brother's mule."

Faith felt a deep sadness wash over her. "Bentley says he didn't mean to kill her, that she fell and drowned when they were arguing out there."

"He certainly planned the meeting with his sister, even made sure her dog couldn't help her," the chief remarked. "And he did nothing to assist her after she fell. Hamlin didn't either. He said she was already dead and there was nothing he could do."

"We never would have guessed when we saw him along the shore road," Brooke said, wrinkling her nose. "He's a pretty good actor."

"There's likely more to his story, but I'm inclined to believe him. Hamlin knew his life was in danger because Smythe thought he'd betrayed him. We caught up with him at the airport, and, as they say in bad films, he sang like a canary." Garris smiled wryly.

"All this time illegal jade was hidden right here at the manor. But we thought someone was after the historical documents." Faith turned to the chief. "Have the analysts come to a conclusion about the documents yet?"

"They were unable to verify their authenticity. It appears that Miss Smythe was not related to Emily Dickinson after all."

Though Faith wasn't surprised, another wave of sadness washed over her at the thought of Emilie's adamant claims turning out to be unfounded.

"Hamlin and Smythe were both looking for the jade," Garris continued. "Smythe arranged for Gnome to search Maggie Haggedorn's bait shop, thinking it had been passed to her." He frowned at Faith.

"According to her, you and Eileen visited her shop right after Gnome's departure in the course of your so-called investigations."

Eileen shot Faith a glance, and Faith knew that her aunt was thinking of the shotgun Maggie had wielded.

Faith briefly described what had transpired and how Watson had discovered the photograph of Maggie with her arm around Emilie.

"We have Mrs. Haggedorn to thank for confirming Smythe's black-market dealings," the chief went on. "She confessed that she had been out by the water with Miss Smythe before their brother got there. Mrs. Haggedorn wanted to convince her to stop carrying illegal merchandise for him. She was worried that her half sister could be in danger."

Ah, Maggie, Faith thought. *You loved Emilie after all.*

"When Mrs. Haggedorn left, Miss Smythe and her dog were fine, but that's when she lost one of her homemade lures. A little detail you neglected to mention." Chief Garris gave Faith a stern, fatherly look, complete with raised eyebrow.

Before Faith could respond, Marlene announced, "As for the big brute, Mrs. Haggedorn called to inquire about adopting him."

How wonderful that Maggie offered to give the brave Carlo a home. And Faith had to admit it would be nice to be able to visit the sweet old Newfie from time to time. She'd miss him—as would Watson.

The door to the library opened, and one of the staff members carried in a tray loaded with coffee, sandwiches, and a delectable array of small cakes.

Marlene rose and waved the employee forward. "Our friends need refreshment. I hope you made the coffee strong." She glanced at Faith with a humorous light in her eyes. "And I hope you didn't forget the milk for Watson. The rascal's earned it!"

Faith looked around at her friends gathered in the beautiful Castleton Manor library and felt a singular joy. A God-designed joy that gave rhyme and reason to life.

The poet of Amherst might have had the same feeling when she penned the lines that sprang to mind at this moment.

Flags—vex a Dying face—
But the least Fan
Stirred by a friend's Hand—
Cools—like the Rain—

Up to this point, we've been doing all the writing. Now it's *your* turn!

Tell us what you think about this book, the characters, the bad guy, or anything else you'd like to share with us about this series. We can't wait to hear from *you*!

Log on to give us your feedback at:
https://www.surveymonkey.com/r/CastletonLibrary

Annie's FICTION